I0738227

Hybrid Vigils

Andrés García Londoño

Translated from the Spanish by Taylor Brady

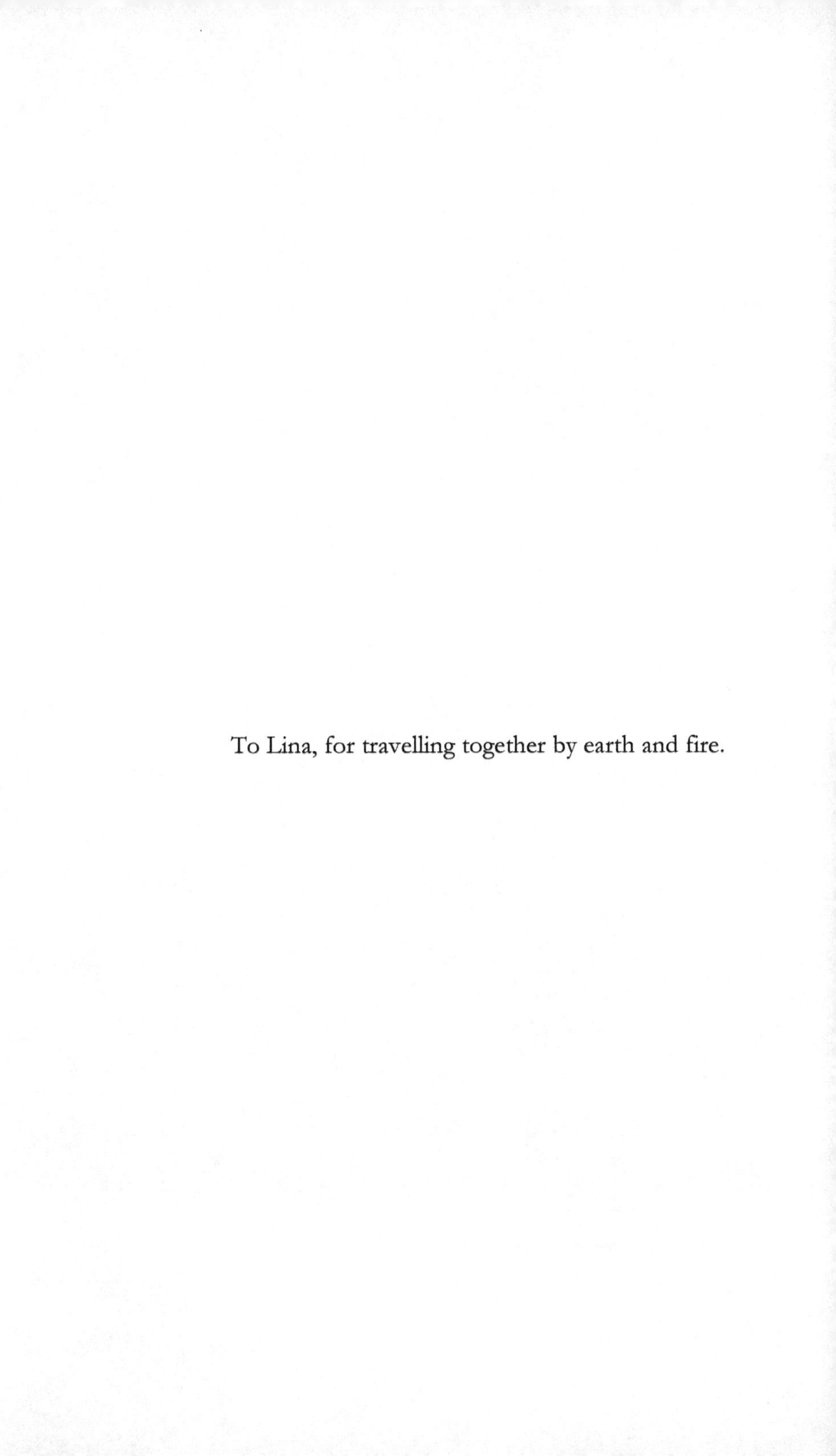

To Lina, for travelling together by earth and fire.

TABLE OF CONTENTS

PROLOGUE

A return to the classics, for Marguerite Yourcenar, consists simply of modernizing the past. This was the direction she took in *Fires*. Her Phaedra wanders the halls of the metro, her Clytemnestra soliloquizes amidst the conflict between Greece and Turkey in the first decades of the twentieth century, and her Sappho is immersed in an atmosphere reminiscent of a variety show or Shakespearean comedy. Albert Camus also traveled this road when he wrote *The Myth of Sisyphus*, ruminating on suicide and the absurd in times of fascism. So did Julio Cortázar, in his poetic drama *The Kings*, where the Minotaur is not a slavering beast, but rather the artist who triumphs over authoritarian power. This preoccupation, that of bringing myths to life in our times, is the successful framework that sustains *Hybrid Vigils*, by Andrés García Londoño.

The title of this book indicates its most disquieting feature. It involves returning to the past, of course, but the essential intent is to explore the ambiguous, striated bedrock of human nature. Andrés García knows that man is the monster and that the beast inhabits him perpetually. He knows, too, that palpitating within every oddity is the shadow of death and the burden of solitude that it imposes. The characters of these stories are mixed beings, shaken by the eccentricity of feeling incomplete, anomalous, ugly. Some of them emerge from fabulous and fantastic universes. And what they ultimately strive to relate is not just their own suffering, but rather the suffering of contemporary humanity. The harpy of these stories shows the dark reality that emerges when love interlaces itself with torture. The Gorgon, a modern plague that annihilates all, describes the terror of the civilized world when faced with apocalyptic destruction. The Sphinx may be stuck in Thebes, but her ancient craving for riddles which was sated by Oedipus has now intensified into a totalitarian thirst for information that none can quench.

Hybrid Vigils sows a universe of mutations that is irrigated by a brimming imagination. Such creative excess would perhaps be unwelcome if it were not balanced by the necessary inquiries that the narrators of these stories launch into their own phantoms and manias, their own vices and eccentricities. Standing out from among deformed centaurs, smitten harpies, invincible Gorgons, lunatic cyclopes, infamous Blemmyes, and computerized Sphinxes is the melancholy and terrifying humanity of the vampire and the butterfly man. These two are the supreme creatures of this book. The depth of their solitude, the despair of their immortality, the wicked irony with which they unravel yarns from the labyrinthine fears of waking and dreams, ensure that their stories will stand vigil in the memory of readers forever. I do not hesitate to declare "The Eyes of the Night" and "The Butterfly Man" the finest stories of *Hybrid Vigils*, a book that even now, for its brilliant strangeness, stands fantastically alone in the panorama of Colombian fiction.

Pablo Montoya Campuzano
Medellín, August 7th, 2009

TRANSLATOR'S NOTE

A little over ten years ago I traveled along the Tambopata River into Bahuaja-Sonene National Park on the very eastern slopes of the Andes Mountains into the Amazon basin: territory that is formally part of Peru and Bolivia, though the borders of nation-states seem utterly absurd amid the incessant animal clamor and humid heat of that rainforest. One night, at the Posada Amazonas eco-lodge, three of the local workers gave a presentation to us gringos about the history of the lodge network (there were a number of others along the river, three of which we stayed at during our journey) and its partnership with the Ese Eja people in and around Puerto Maldonado. The employees were presenting in English, their third language after Ese Eja and Spanish, and in certain sections the words came in fits and starts. Most of the small audience was patient, and helped the workers find the words where we could, but there were a number of those who, vocally and in the middle of the presentation, expressed disgust at the unmitigated gall of the locals to present to us in anything other than flawless English.

The real shamelessness on display, that of the Americans' disdain, prompted those of us fluent enough in Spanish to speak with and apologize to the workers after the presentation was over, and to ask them more about their lives.

English is often wielded as a bulldozer to denude the landscapes of voices in places which Anglophone people have colonized. Languages as diverse as Gaeilge, O'Odham, Malayalam, Gĩkũyũ, even Spanish have been suppressed at the insistence of people on the fundamental inferiority of those tongues and the people who speak them, on the primacy of English. Yet English as we speak it now, and indeed all living languages, are nothing if not memories of the myriad people who speak and have spoken them. Even in that last sentence, we have words like 'myriad' (which arrived to English via French, via Latin, via Greek) mixed in with 'speak', 'we', 'now' (from Old English via Proto-Germanic), and 'memories', which arrives to us more directly from Anglo-Norman French and Latin. There is multiplicity aestivating within all languages, perhaps most of all—ironically—within colonial tongues.

It is precisely that multiplicity of our language which indicated to me that translation into English was a fitting fate for these brilliant stories about hybrid beings. I found them myself almost eight years ago among the mountains of volumes populating a tiny bookshop in Medellín close to the bus station for Parque Arví. Even there, paralyzed by the treasure hoard before me and the logistics of cramming as much of it into my luggage as possible without throwing out all my clothes, I knew I would bring home *Relatos Híbridos*, as this book is titled in Spanish. As I tried to merely skim its contents I found myself engrossed, reading through much of the book while two of my friends dozed in the evening breeze on the steps outside.

What captivated my attention was how seamlessly Andrés' writing transfused myth into the body of the quotidian, and the quotidian into the body of myth. These characters' fantastic surroundings and experiences only make them seem more real, their humanity more anguishing. It can be easy to treat myths as canonical texts, ancient and remote, or enshrined in the "best" translations that cannot be changed or reinterpreted lest the stories lose their power. Yet that reverence misapprehends both the role which myth serves and the linguistic vehicles by which myth has been made available to us throughout time. Such tales have always contextualized the persistent mysteries which we face in living, and they have always been retold and translated, their universes expanded to encompass new scenarios as the era demands.

Evolution, that life of a myth which continues to reveal new truths about ourselves, is what determines its durability. That said, it takes a skilled mind to conceive of a new realm into which a myth may inquire, and it is for this reason that I am drawn strongly to the story "A Question of No Future". It centers on the Sphinx, re-imagined as a computer so enormous and powerful that it must eventually be housed deep within the ocean as a heat sink. At her creators' behest, the Sphinx begins her own inquiries into foundational science, yielding immense benefits for the development of new technologies. She then proceeds through economics, politics, and finally into the intimate worlds of human affairs and psychology, optimizing all the way. Yet it is when humanity knows the most that they realize how much they have abdicated, how many fulfilling paths have been foreclosed by their insistence on living according to the Sphinx's ruthless calculations, her singular interpretations. Particularly salient to our lives now, the greatest mystery is knowledge that we have but do not actually understand.

***

For much of that summer I went to Colombia, two friends of mine had lived in Medellín seeking some rarefied knowledge: making new friends, learning as much Spanish as possible, dancing most nights, reading most days. Yet when another pal and I arrived to visit them, they still felt that there was a level on which they did not understand and were not relating to the people they met. They had a view through windows into the outer rooms of the home but no invitation to step over the threshold.

A few days into my time there, we were fortunate enough to have a conversation with a student from Eafit University near where we were staying. Responding to our inquiry about the reticence of many Colombians that my friends had met, she illuminated that—for her at least—it stemmed from a self-consciousness accrued as armor against the reductive views of foreigners toward Colombians—views which are usually distilled from the narrowest interpretation of the worst aspects of recent Colombian history that have received disproportionate coverage in the international press and schlocky television shows. Armor against the notion that Colombian people are a category, and a monstrous one at that, thus devaluing the majority of their lives, including their very real and persistent struggles. I feel confident that this conversation would not have taken place, certainly not the revelatory turn it took, if we had been speaking English. What was critical to the depth of that discussion was that the Anglophone interlocutors met our partner where she was, that we inhabited the other self that new languages introduce to our consciousness.

This seems a corrosive, self-defeating thought for a translator to express to readers when introducing literature that is presented monolingually, in English only, that is conspicuously not in its original form, and thus could seem to imply that the reader is not meeting the Spanish text where it is and thereby missing out on much of its profundity. That is not my intent, but if I can make a small request of the reader beyond the graciousness they have shown in sticking with me thus far, it is that they consider the hybrid nature of our own language, its myriad past and (I hope) its complex future. Indeed so much of contemporary English has affinities with or is cognate with Spanish, that it seems a shame for us not to peruse more closely what we think we already know in order to discover that which we did not, and I have embraced this principle wholeheartedly while translating Andrés' wonderful prose. We are not sublimated whole and pure from a messy universe. We are not one thing, but many, and the words to describe that experience are never very far away.

Taylor Brady
Redwood City, February 21st, 2021

Hybrid Vigils

HARPY'S MILK

Am I ugly? The water, mirroring the torchlight in the darkness of the cavern, returns my face's reflection. A twisted image; almost illegible. My sisters have abandoned me from fear of our masters, but as I look at myself I see them. This withered face, littered with scars and ravined with wrinkles, this face of millennia, is also theirs. What difference is there between us?... The more that I look at myself, the less I understand how he could have come to love me.

I know women's bodies well from having dismembered thousands of them, and I understand what little separates us in this regard: my wings, my back covered with feathers, the talons at the ends of my hands and feet. But in other respects, the difference is enormous, and in nothing more so than in our age. They are all mere children. I, on the other hand, am old. As old as the world? I do not know; my memories are vast, but they do not reach back to my birth. Even so... one time I had to attend to a philosopher. I learned much while I worked on him. He had sought wisdom, and he complained that he had not lived long enough to achieve it. If he knew what I have seen, he would have understood that it is the same to live for a day as to live for a thousand years, and that ignorance is a condition intrinsic to existence. I did not tell him this, however. It would have alleviated his suffering… and my job is to do the opposite.

Now I only have sisters, but I do not believe that it was always this way. In my most remote memories there are also brothers. That male of our species who I see carrying me in the oldest of these recollections, is he my father? When I recall my childhood, I confront a distinct emotion, one without parallel in any memory of my life besides those of the few hours of love that I myself have striven to wipe away. I believe that our victims, men, call this emotion happiness. And our first task is to snatch that from them.

I remember little from the day the Titans came. Everyone was asleep after a night of work, which I imagine made the massacre easy. What could we do against the creators of our own universe? Nevertheless, I believe that there were those who fought, because I recall bellows, and not just cries of fright. But, I repeat, what could we do against an army of all-powerful giants?… There were flames. I remember. Many fires. And finally, the earthquake which swallowed what was left of the village. In the aftermath what rules my memories is the odor of burnt flesh… of the burnt flesh of my mother. And the weight of the chains that they placed on all of the girls, as well as the pain when they yanked out our feathers so that we could not escape. But everything is muddled until I encounter the first clear image: that of my sisters, chained in a line and led forth by the giants. The Titans' guffaws, the tears of my sisters, my tears. Soon we would learn not to cry. That very night, when they raped us and afterward ripped out our tongues.

Upon our arrival, hell was empty. But the Titans decided to create man and from before he was even born, they had conceived how to punish him. They installed us here. We were the first inhabitants of Hades, and while we waited for the first of the dead, our captors taught us how to treat them. We learned, with delight, the art of torture. Our repressed rage even allowed us to develop new techniques, since those of the Titans were too blatant. They only thought of dismembered limbs, burnt eyeballs, and nails sinking into flesh. We preferred subtlety. Only the ordinary dead deserved a punishment as graceless as our talons sinking into their bodies or our shrieks bursting their eardrums. The demigods merited special treatment, as did the infamous mortals who for their sins had fallen under Hades' jurisdiction. Treatment such as that we gave to Prometheus. Every morning while he lay chained to a rock, it was one of us who ripped out his liver, not an eagle, as some dim-witted chronicler recorded. It was me, in fact, who had the idea that the organ would regrow every day, and I was tasked with preparing the regenerative potion.

Yes, the Titans were wise to choose us as guardians of the underworld. After all, what man could conceive the torture of Sisyphus? It requires intelligence to think of this, not just power. Who else but a woman could coax a man to carry a rock up a hill whence it would always roll back down? In the eons that have elapsed since he arrived, it has taken all of our powers of feminine persuasion, cooed in gestures and caresses with our wings when he becomes discouraged, to deceive him for interminable eras into thinking that the torment will cease if he can, just once more, complete his impossible task. We have had to employ all our wiles to make promises that we have known from the start we would not have to fulfill… Perhaps it was for this reason that the Titans captured only us, and sacrificed our brothers: they would have been too blatant when the time came to express their hatred toward all of existence.

When the Titans fell and were replaced by the gods, little changed for us. It was a coup, not a revolution. History was rewritten, of course, and new plans proposed, so we may never know the destiny that their original creators had in mind for the Cosmos. But the general state of things stayed the same, because the gods saw no reason to change what functioned best in the universe: hell itself. The new managers—I remember thinking of this while working on a stock trader whom I made eat the bills and coins that he had made during life— simply installed one of their own as the new administrator, but kept all of the personnel. The only real difference for us was that afterward we could count among our prisoners those who had initially enslaved us. In the deepest corner of Tartarus, the primordial giants were chained to the same roots as the tectonic plates, so that when one of them tried to free themselves, it would cause an earthquake. At first, we would go down to torture them, stabbing our wings into their giant lidless eyes, but later we ceased our visits altogether. As I said: we are subtle. Once we comprehended that nothing could be more terrible for an almighty being than a monotonous eternity spent in darkness, we deprived them even of the relief of a change of routine, though that change be painful and last only for a single day.

I have seen everything. Or so I believed until recently. I have been witness to the villainy of mankind and the parsimony of the gods, great misers who intend to monopolize destiny for all eternity. And without destiny, what riches have any value? At some point in eternity, these eyes have seen every human sin, every divine indolence. Through my talons have passed artists, teachers, soldiers, lawyers, politicians… and they have brought little new each time. In general, the human species is no better than the gods and they rely on excuses no less frequently. But excuses are worth little: in their case as in that of the gods, our world is what we make of it, how we play the cards the fates have dealt us. But it is easier to complain… Ay, this eternal mania of complaining! Do I complain of having been abused, enslaved, and mutilated? No, I do not complain. I simply hate. And for this reason no excuse will ever free anybody from the blade of my talons… Clearly, I should confess that I too have my weaknesses: if I have to attend to a woman, I cannot avoid feeling a certain sympathy, a certain solidarity. I pour the hot oil on her, I thrust the daggers in her, I burn her; yes, of course, it is my function; but rarely do I mess with her mind. And I know that my sisters do the same. In general, women fare better than men in the inferno. We know what they have gone through and as a result, in spite of everything, we tend to grant them the benefit of the doubt.

There is no silence in my world. Always cries. Neverending. Usually they are little more than ambient noise. No more than the sound of a river for somebody who lives nearby. Yet there are days when the complete lack of silence weighs on you, because we recall our incapacity to break the silence ourselves. Little by little, my sisters and I have been able to overcome the absence of our tongues with our own language based on variations in our inarticulate shrieks. In this way, we can communicate our basic experiences from a distance. A "Heads Up!" if one of the gods comes down to supervise our torturous labors, as if we were slacking office workers alerting one another to the arrival of the boss. Or a "Come help me!" in the improbable event that one of the dead resists their torment. We have known how to read for a long time, of course, thanks to one of Odysseus' companions. Also, a pedophilic professor was courteous enough to teach us sign language while he was seated on the stake that we had prepared specially so that his own weight would slowly impale him. But these are all just coarse approximations: there is nothing that can replace normal speech. Nothing that can truly break the silence. Nothing that can distance us from our minds which are always giving birth to words, always occupied, always dammed up. Because words do not cease being born simply because the organ to express them is missing. And for us, words, having no way to escape, slowly putrefy within us. Never spoken concurrent with their context, words fester like an infection, starting from the scar on our severed tongues, spreading to the esophagus and thence to the rest of the body, until it is saturated with rot.

Never more so than now, however, have I felt the weight of the silence. He was a soldier, like so many others that had visited us, although a little younger than the majority. He had died in his second battle, but already during his first he had committed a sin great enough to bring him here. Witness to the massacre of a village of peasants, he had done nothing to stop it. His cowardice brought him here. Although in death he showed none of the lack of valor that condemned him in life. I ask myself, what would they say of him, the scales held by the grand arbiter in which each soul is weighed after crossing the river, if he were weighed again today?... But the question is useless: there is nothing left to weigh anymore.

I saw nothing exceptional about him when I met him. I confess. Nothing alerted me, at least not consciously. He was just another of the dead. And like any other spirit I gave him flesh only to make him suffer, using the standard protocol for such cases. I slowly reviewed the horrors that each one of the victims suffered and made a list. The idea behind the method was simple: make him experience with his own flesh each one of the agonies caused by his comrades. I threw myself into the task. With help from the cyclopes I made him relive the terror of a hundred rapes; Cerberus subjected him to a dozen dis-memberments; the maggots ate him alive just as they had de-voured the survivors. But he went through all of this without it affecting him. He cried out, of course, every time that a dog sunk its canines into him and ripped off a chunk of flesh. He howled as the gaffs penetrated his chest and hoisted him, sep-arating his trunk from his legs to show him the meaning of rootlessness. He squealed like a pig about to be slaughtered when we closed him in the mold replete with razors to show him the meaning of having internal scars that disfigure you... but his cries were merely a result of the physical pain, and he passed from one torture to another as an empty shell would, like a golem that would only wake up to scream when it was tortured. I did not see him demonstrate genuine pain. Not the pain that we seek. Not the pain of terror. Not the pain of fearing that something will occur again.

Our intention with such procedures is always simple. Make the tortured reach the greatest pain: that of self-loathing. To recognize one's essential foulness by experiencing with one's own flesh the pain that one has caused. In his case, then, we were failing. How could we achieve what we wanted with him? When I ran out of ideas, I sought counsel during the weekly work meeting with my sisters. Obviously this is the most silent work meeting that you could imagine, because all communication is written. But it is effective: our collective knowledge of the most apt way to torture the condemned surpasses the inventiveness of any one of us. When I presented the case, one of my sisters told me that, judging by a Nazi commander that she had once tortured, I may have been searching in vain for a fitting physical torment. She recommended that I break away from the obvious: make him experience the massacre with his own eyes.

So I did. I prepared everything. With needle and thread I sewed the soldier's eyelids to his brow and placed him in stocks before a mirror. With his own blood and the blood of one of the victims, also in our possession for a sin committed prior to the massacre, I brewed a potion to recall the event in which the two had encountered each other, and spread it onto the mirror. Thanks to the blood's memory, he was able to see the scene once again, just as he had seen it for the first time: with his own eyes. The arrival in the village, the orders, the screams, the flames, the rapes, the executions, the mutilations; I thought to include even the way his hands were stained by the smoke. And when the scene had finished, I appreciated anew the accumulated wisdom of our thousands of years of work with the most monstrous of humans. The soldier cried like a child, whining and sobbing. I knew, then, why the regular procedure had been unsuccessful. I had sought to create a self-loathing that already lay within him. It was not necessary to teach him to see the world through the eyes of his victims; it was worse for him to see it with his own eyes. I did not have to instill guilt in him; he already carried the burden of knowing that he was a coward in the most decisive moment of his life. And upon seeing that he loathed himself, I felt the pleasure of being able to loathe him for it. I departed, leaving everything ready so that the scene could be repeated over and over again.

When I returned the next day, he was much the same, although his eyes had already started to shed tears of blood. Knowing well that in the long run, psychological torture ceases to be effective if there is no break or preparation for the next session, such as Sisyphus has while descending the mountain after his rock, I untied him and prepared to take care of him myself. I laid him out on a narrow table, tied him up, and asked myself what to do with him, how to distract him until giving him his next dose of traumatic memory. I do not really know why I did it—at the time it seemed logical to me without really thinking about it, although now I can not think of a reason— but I chose to give him a treatment generally set aside for rapists. I armed my wingtips' plumage with steel blades, sat astride him all tied up, and embraced him, burying my face into his neck and letting my feathers sink into his back and thorax… Until that point everything had been normal. But the silence that followed was not. Intrigued, I lifted my gaze and saw his face. His eyes watched me and amidst all the wounds, I focused on their color. They were brownish-grey, with a brightness that perturbed me. Had I already felt it? "What am I doing sitting on top of him?" I asked myself. I felt confused. And what that man did then simply exacerbated the sensation. He opened his mouth and every holdfast of mine was shaken.

"How beautiful you are," he said.

Just that. Four words for my entire past to be cast into doubt. I did not know what to do. I got up. I looked at him. And I felt an enormous rage. Who was he to mock me? Furious, I lashed him once more to the stocks, left him to contemplate the same scene as always, the most important and terrible of his life, and went to attend to more of the condemned, whom I treated more brutally than ever before. Even so, I could not stop thinking about the soldier the entire day. With an immense fury, yes, but muddled with another emotion that I could not precisely define… as well as a great anxiety.

The next day I could not contain myself. I went to his torture chamber and untied him. While I looked at him with ire and pondered what to do with him, he returned my gaze expectantly. There were no more tears in his eyes: the scene of the massacre had ceased to have an effect on him. Finally, perhaps because I did not really know what else to do, or perhaps because I was too curious, I tied him again to the table and sat astride him, making sure to sink the blades on my wings deep into his flesh so that he did not get any ideas. But instead of crying out, he whispered just loud enough to hear:

"I feared that I would not see you again."

This time, the blades were not enough: I sunk my talons into the skin of his shoulders until I felt them strike bone. But he did not cry out. Nor did I stop. Instead, he pressed himself against me as much as his restraints would allow, and I sunk my talons deeper into him, feeling how the bone fractured. We stayed this way for a long time. The more that I wounded him, the more it affected me. The more it confused me. The more it became clear to me. Finally his contact became unbearable: it represented too many truths all bundled together. Exhausted, I got up, untied him, and carried him to the stocks. He let me do this without resisting. Once he was bound, I contemplated him intently for an instant, as if I myself feared that I would not see him again. The rest of that day it was exceedingly diffi-cult for me to concentrate. Something had taken up residence within me. Something that grew, that burned me more deeply than the boiling oil that I poured over each and every one of the condemned until it seared their exposed bones.

When I returned the following day, the scene was exactly the same. But this time, he only said two words.

"Kiss me."

Which two words could sound more filthy in hell? Which expression contain a more atrocious petition? I did not yield to his desire. Yet I had already admitted to myself that I thrilled to feel his body against my own. His chest beneath my breasts. His breath against my neck. His member against my vulva, both palpitating and swollen, separated only by his infernal prisoner's garb. I sunk my talons into him with sick delight… Until that moment, sex for me had only been the memory of the night of my rape. The specter of the Titans, who had debased their bodies and assailed us, just little girls, their presence like a fog that surrounds, obscures, contaminates, erases everything. All innocence. All well-being. All light. This was different. His body appeared to shine, and as he lit up, so did I.

I do not know how I managed to separate myself from him. Not that day, nor the next, nor the next. And even less still, when a week later he changed his usual remark. Instead of asking me for something, he made a declaration, a simple confirmation of the state of things.

"I love you."

This drove me crazy. I could think of nothing else except returning to him and laying myself across his body. And, as with every pair of truly passionate lovers, we were careless. I could count on the solidarity of my sisters, who looked at me with a mixture of alarm, confusion, and curiosity, but not on the thousand other minions who comprise the rest of the personnel in Hades. I knew that they whispered about me in the corners of the dungeons, that it was only a matter of time until the gods found out and separated us. Love is the only sin that Hades can not accommodate.

Meanwhile, I tried to prolong the situation as much as I could, disguising our encounters as torture. Or could it be that sex always has some element of torture? Perhaps I was already too set in my ways to change completely? I know quite well that in Hades, eros must be expressed in the most perverse way possible, but I recall my talons in his flesh and I don't know…

The truth is that I don't know if it was necessary to wound him so much. To what extent did I torture him simply because that was already part of my nature? To what extent did his declaration strengthen my refusal to give him a kiss? Ten millennia of subtlety will shape anybody: in what worse way could you torture someone in love than by denying their request for a form of contact that unambiguously expresses your own delight? Truthfully, I do not really know who wanted to make him suffer. Was it the harpy? The woman? Or simply the feminine?

I do know, though, who took action when I found out, thanks to one of my sisters, that the administrative decision had already been made and that they would separate me from him forever. That day I stretched myself across him and ground myself with such desperation against his body as if I were trying to erase the borders of our flesh. When I finished, still feeling how my vulva pulsed, I was exhausted and began to cry. Taken aback and still tied up, he kissed my tears and spoke at greater length than he ever had.

"I also love your pain, but you have no reason to cry. I must tell you something: I only regretted one thing about having died and that was that nobody should die without having loved someone besides himself. You have cured me of that. As a result, whatever happens, everything is beautiful. Everything is alright."

What could I do before such a declaration? Before such youth? Before such naïveté with respect to what would happen to him when they separated us? Perhaps only one thing. What I did. I lifted my breast to his mouth and, smiling at him for the first time, asked him to drink. Harpy's milk. Milk of children who will never be born. Milk of a race that is already extinct, despite the fact that my sisters and I still live, since we can never procreate. Cursed? Blessed? In either case, we are the only ones able to create that powerful liquid, capable of achieving what no potion or magical brew can. I shuddered with pleasure as he drank, and I cried and smiled and clumsily caressed his hair. Well, my talons were accustomed to very different labors.

When he finished drinking, his body began to dissolve into vapors that would flow through the entire Cosmos. Or, what is one and the same, that would never be reunited in one place. He would never again exist. For an instant he looked at me in surprise, but quickly his expression changed to comprehension. My beloved was smiling in thanks for the gift that only a harpy can give: Oblivion. Definitive dissolution. The ultimate escape. All that remained were the empty table and the lost shadow of his smile.

Once more I was alone, but this time it hurt, and I have never been the same.

***

My sin is too great to be forgiven. Nevertheless, how could they punish me? Only through him could they have made me suffer, but I beat them to him.

"What to do with her?" I imagine them asking. I have become someone that they cannot trust, yet the entire structure of Hades depends on the harpies. Each one of us is too precious and irreplaceable to sacrifice us flippantly and risk, if not an open rebellion of my sisters, then without a doubt their undying disdain, and the resulting loss of productivity. And the gods continue where they are in large part because the underworld has always run like a clock. One could accuse them of many things, perhaps, but not of stupidity. They know quite well whom they need.

Perhaps for these reasons, the menace of punishment has loomed only on these fronts: in threat and in isolation. I think that my sisters avoid me not just for fear of falling into disgrace themselves; I also believe that they fear becoming corrupted with my confusion.

What is left for me? Certainly I cannot follow in my lover's footsteps, since I am immune to the effects of the milk of my race. Neither can I return to being a good torturer... Who, once they know what it truly means to love a body, can rip apart even one more?

Escape? To where?

All of this has convinced me that there is no better place for me than in my memories. I have lived for millennia but still, my mind always circles around those same scant days. Yet my solitude is not unbearable because, even if my isolation never ends and I have to spend forever in this cavern until time itself ends, thanks to him I will never be unaccompanied. In fact, of all that occurred, I only lament never having acceded to his request to kiss him. I gave him everything else: yes, all of the passion, every intimate touch between bodies, but not that. Not the most basic, not the simplest... I do not know why I resisted. I do not know if it was my way of maintaining control or if it was simply fear. But none of the rest, none of what we did, is anything that I can find regrettable. His gaze has snuck inside of me. Now, seeing myself reflected in the water, the doubt surges.

How could I regret anything that happened, when in place of an eternity of hell I now have a happy memory to relive until the end of time? He sowed the seed and I intend to nurture it, returning to him again and again. It could be that my solitude has not changed, but it is better than what I had before: now there is something in my loneliness besides the inferno.

Besides, there is something else… Is it faith or a strange form of madness that I feel growing, stronger every day, inside of me?… Yes, it must be faith. Faith in the end. Illogical, irrational, like all faith. Yet even if it is simply madness, it does not matter. No, it does not matter: what matters is that I believe.

What I feel, what I think, is that there will come a day when a new conflict between the almighty beings will crumple up the cosmos like a discarded paper bag, and what I sense, what I even foolishly hope, is that by that time I will have remembered him so perfectly that he will return to me whole and possess me completely. On that day all that is imperfect will be erased. On that day the world will be remade. On that day, both of us will partake of my milk and we will find it sweet.

On that day there will only be kisses.

On that day I will find myself beautiful.

And from my milk, the Cosmos will be reborn.

THE CYCLOPS AND THE MOON

Shen Xiao, a young Chinese poet of verses that were not very good but were nonetheless sensitive and daring, did something rather unoriginal that many before him had done: he fell in love with the moon. After that moment he would stay awake every night gazing at his beloved. We could say that he slept during the day if that were not actually false, since, like any good lover he spent his days with insomnia, awaiting only the moment when he could see the white goddess once again. In this manner, night after night, he came to know his beloved and would ask himself questions about her. One question, above all others, intrigued him: why did the moon have to wane for thirteen days of every month? Why could she not always stay full, brilliant, radiant, and happy? Because it seemed to Shen, who was so tangled up with the moon, that she was unhappy as she waned. And this unhappiness hurt him as if the pain were his own, so that he asked himself if there was anything he could do to alleviate it.

That he was obsessively enamored with the moon could be explained by the fact that Shen was not a man with a regular appearance. He stood more than a hand's-breadth over two meters in a country where the average stature is much smaller. Yet his differences did not end there, because in his earliest infancy he had suffered a horrific accident. While he was wrapped in silk sheets in his crib, during a drought which had devastated the countryside, a famished raven had plucked out one of his eyes.

His stature and the appearance of his empty eye socket, over which extended an immobile eyelid, had condemned him since childhood to be considered absolutely hideous and to never encounter a woman who would love him. Perhaps for this reason he chose, as object of his affection, the most lofty that he could find. And his loneliness brought him to do something that was indeed original: although many before him had become enamored with the moon, he was the first one to decide to seek her out. Money was no object since he was a member of the mandarin class. So he spent his entire fortune to acquire the best boat and best crew available, with the intention of going to the ends of the earth to find the moon's abode. He retained only a shop selling jade vases to take care of his widowed mother, who from that point on wept all day long and dressed all in white to mourn her dead son.

He knew that to reach his objective he had to head west, where the sun set, past the shores of all known lands and carrying on even further. Regarding the vicissitudes of the journey, to enumerate them all would be another nearly interminable tale, so we shall say little of them here. Suffice it to say that he traversed the known world: from his vantage at sea he saw the mysteries of the Indian jungles, the tropics and deserts of Africa, and the frozen seas to the south. But shortly after skirting the black continent and just before passing the Pillars of Hercules and continuing his journey into an unexplored ocean, he was attacked by a ship of pirates descended from Greek colonists and as a result lost not just his crew and his vessel, but also his right arm—the one that he wrote with—when he was wounded with an arrow and then attacked by a shark while he floated in the water after the shipwreck. The pirates, impressed by his height, recovered him from the sea, cured his wounds, and spared his life, because it amused them to have a one-eyed giant as a slave; and, ignorant of his language and thus unable to communicate with him, they dubbed him Polyphemus. Rebaptized as a cyclops, Shen suffered for a few months the misfortunes of slavery until a storm dragged the pirate ship too far west, where it was attacked by a giant sea serpent, which are abundant in the far reaches of the earth. It was then, after navigating alone for a few days on the flotsam of the shipwreck, sustaining himself with gulls and fish, that Shen reached the end of the world.

The old tales were true. The furious ocean hurled itself over the border of the flat world of Shen Xiao, falling interminably into the cosmic blackness where the stars hove into view within the vapor. Only a giant white castle, with features as delicate as they were imposing, interrupted the chaos of the waters. Shen swam that direction as well as he could with his single arm, and not merely to save his own life while the timbers on which he had floated hurtled into the void, but rather because he suspected that he had arrived at his destination: the abode of his beloved. When he reached the castle, right at the point where the sea met the astral abyss, he walked for a few meters and leaned over the border: below lay the eternal emptiness and, for a moment, Shen Xiao thought he glimpsed the carapace of the great turtle on whose back the world is situated. But he could not control the vertigo that the emptiness produced in him, and he had not come to look at the turtle, so he immediately turned around and searched for the entrance to the house of the moon.

The gates were so big that an entire regiment could have passed through them with each soldier standing atop the shoulders of the last. It took Shen hours to get inside the palace. The first thing that he realized when he arrived at the patio beyond the foyer was that he could satisfy his hunger from the shipwreck and never have to worry about sustenance while he was there. Practically everything in the palace of the moon was edible and everything, absolutely everything, was white. The floor tiles on which he stood were made of hard cheese; the fountain in the garden—which from the dwarfed perspective of Shen Xiao was like the tallest cataract—flowed with pure milk; the wall's bricks were grains of rice as big as the poet himself. So, after taking advantage of the fact that it had grown dark and consequently that the occupants should not be around, he sought to orient himself and find her room. It was almost dawn when he discovered it and took refuge behind a curtain of white silk to surreptitiously contemplate the arrival of the moon.

His beloved was much more beautiful—and more gigantic—than Shen had thought. When the moon moved her enormous body, the fabric of her dress created currents of air that the poet felt as great gusts, for which reason he had to clutch the curtain so as not to risk being swept away by what was for him little less than a typhoon. Yet the gale-force aroma of her celestial body was more stirring than the union of all of the flowers in all of the gardens of all of the emperors of China since the world had been turning. He had to say, indeed, that the moon was younger than he had imagined: in human years she would have been little more than ten. Only one thing in the moon's body did not correspond to what one would expect from any mere child, but rather belonged to a much greater entity: her eyes showed the intelligence of somebody who is one with eternity. What's more, her beauty was difficult to describe. Every part of her was white, but in multiple shades. Her hair, her brows, and her eyes, for example, were of a white so dark that they appeared black in comparison to her skin; her lips, pinkish when compared to the porcelain that surrounded them. So bright were her light and the perfection of every movement, every feature, that Shen Xiao feared more than once that beholding such a spectacle he would lose vision in his only remaining eye. Nevertheless he kept looking, his love being greater than his fear of blindness.

The moon began to read from a book as big as a tower which was supported by a lectern at the foot of the bed. When, after a long time, she finally went to sleep, Shen stayed awake watching her spellbound until, shortly before nightfall, the exhaustion of his adventures and his latest shipwreck overtook him. He awoke after the moon had already gone, and was still so tired that he simply ate part of a rice grain almost his same size which he had detached from the wall, and went back to sleep. When he awoke again, he realized that he was thirsty, and so he went toward the bathroom in search of something to drink. There he discovered that the moon had bathed before her departure and that, when she had risen from the tub, drops of milk with an aroma of jasmine had fallen from her body, each one creating a puddle which the poet could cross only by jumping. Shen Xiao scooped up some of the milk with his hand and drank it. Suddenly aware that the milk he drank had touched the skin of the one he loved, a shiver ran through him, so painfully thrilling that he thought never again in his life would he experience such pleasure. Then he scooped all the milk that he could into the canteen hung from his belt.

When the moon returned, Shen realized immediately that something had changed. She was no longer a child. She was a young adolescent and her body began to show the roundness that announced the arrival of womanhood. She read for a couple of hours and Shen Xiao, finding her more attractive now that she was not a child, contemplated her in ecstasy until the moon went to bed.

For ten days the cycle repeated. Every time that she returned, the moon was a few years older. And every time she was more beautiful. And Shen Xiao fell more deeply in love. But on the eleventh day there was a change. The arrival of the moon, more brilliant than ever, flooded the room for a moment with whiteness. At first Shen could see nothing in such light; he was blinded before his eye could adapt and see that a forty-year old had entered the room. But this time she did not read. She sat down to write. She did this with magic: waving her hand from which symbols streamed onto what always seemed to be the last page of the book that she had previously returned to read, but each time that she turned the page, a new one appeared. Something else was different. In contrast to the moon that he had come to know, serene and at times happy, this new moon was serious, even sad. And when she went to bed, she cried until she fell asleep.

Shen Xiao could not bear it. So he decided to carry out an idea that had been coalescing in his mind for a few days. Determined, he headed toward the bed and, with difficult pirouettes using his only arm, he began to scale the edge of the sheet. Nightfall found him with a quarter of the bed still left to climb, so due to the earthquake that the moon caused when she arose, he nearly plummeted to the ground from a height many times greater than that necessary to kill him. When Shen reached the top, he was so spent that he was barely able to drag himself to the edge of the pillow and hide beneath one of its tips where he figured that the moon's head would not smash him when she laid down to rest. Her arrival found him sleeping, but the shaking caused by her great body upon reclining in the bed awoke him. He waited until she fell asleep after crying and then left his hiding place to observe her face from closer up. All night he gazed, her head occupying his entire field of view, filling the entire world, replacing it. A thousand poems that he did not record occurred to Shen just contemplating how the moon's nose twitched while inhaling each breath.

The following day he occupied himself figuring out how to survive in the bed, aware that although he did not want to stay there, he did not have the strength to descend and ascend once more. So he moved close to the wall and ate some rice. He was worried about finding fluids to slake his thirst, but then he remembered the crying. He climbed the hill of the pillow and, placing his hand between the fibers, recovered some of the moisture that the moon's eyes had shed. He then realized that he was mistaken when he thought that drinking the drops of milk which had fallen from the moon's body was the greatest pleasure he would ever experience.

Ten days passed this way. Ten days in which the moon aged and wrote in the book. He wanted to know what it said, but the book remained closed during the day and, given his size, it would take an army of Shen Xiaos to open it. Nevertheless, he had other things to worry about: perhaps it was because of the wisdom he had acquired from drinking the moon's tears—or simply common sense—but Shen Xiao foresaw what would come to pass and it pained him from that point forward. He had something he must do, something so that she would know that she had not been alone in her pain. So he searched for anything with which to write. He found it in an eyelash of the moon that he collected from the pillow. Although it was much larger than he was, he cut off the top end with his mariner's knife and thus made himself a pen. Ink was another problem. And soon enough he realized that there was only one place where he could obtain something that would fulfill that function. So he placed the dagger on the bed and rapidly ran his hand over it, collecting with his canteen the blood that fell from the clean cut. Then he wrapped the wound as well as he could with a fiber from the pillow, using his teeth to help tie the improvised bandage. Now the only thing that worried him was whether he would have enough time to complete his mission before the blindness he felt advancing in his only eye became complete. Like a mountaineer lost in the snow, his retinas were burning and each day his vision grew more blurry. Hence he could not, with impunity, look at the moon every day from only a hand's breadth away.

On the twenty-sixth day after he arrived at the palace of the moon, he did what he had to do. The centenarian moon, her face marred by wrinkles but still as beautiful as ever in Shen's eyes, went to bed after writing. She did not cry this time, however. In her heavy, ancient gaze there was tranquil resignation. And Shen Xiao, trembling, struck by pain that made him exhale in gasps as if his own life were escaping with every breath, anxiously watched the chest rise and fall with every inhalation and exhalation, more slowly each time, until the moment came when it stopped and did not move again.

Death, especially of one we love, always feels final regardless of any other belief or premonition that we may have. What terrifies us is discovering just how alone it reveals us to be. And so Shen Xiao howled with pain and with his only hand yanked out his hair and clawed at his face in despair. Nothing remained in the world for him besides the moon, and for a brief moment he even thought about committing suicide by leaping over the edge of the bed. But he restrained himself and, upon observing that the book had stayed open this time, he realized that it was the perfect moment to put his plan into action.

Aware that he would have not just the day but also the following night to complete his objective, Shen descended the bed and began to climb the lectern. More than once his life was left hanging by a thread—or to be more exact, from his only hand—when he slipped during the ascent, but he reached the book by afternoon of the following day. In spite of the blurriness of his vision, the symbols were so large that he could decipher them. It was, as he had suspected, the book of destiny. Everything was there. Written in white letters on a grey background, every incident from the previous month, every thought of every human being, every experience of every animal or plant were registered there. Everything, absolutely everything that the moon had seen, heard, or intuited during her quotidian journey through the night. Only in her own house did the moon take a break from her omniscience, it seemed. This led Shen Xiao to ask himself how it was that she had not discovered his intention to come visit her. Could it be perhaps that she had thought he died during the journey? Or perhaps, like so many among us, was the moon blind only to those that loved her?

In any case, Shen thought, it was a good place, the best even, to write his message, hoping that she would notice its conspicuous color despite the fact that even if he made the writing larger than himself, it would not reach the size of any of the other symbols. He wrote, then, a poem, whose inexact translation from Mandarin we will publish below:

Hidden in your sheets like an ant
I could admire your secret

After finishing his task, Shen once again descended the lectern and climbed the bed. An entire day and night had passed before he found himself close to his beloved's body and already the metamorphosis of her eternal rebirth was far along. Enclosed in a cocoon of white silk, the moon was growing out of the remains of her own corpse. Shen Xiao held his breath until he began to see the cocoon moving softly, rhythmically. The moon's heart had begun to beat again. So great was Shen Xiao's elation at discovering that his beloved was alive and that the nightmare of her death had not been permanent, that his own heartbeat began to run wild. An unbearable pain that rose pulsing through his left arm indicated that, depending on how you look at it, the effort of climbing the lectern had been too much for him, or that all of his hardships had taken their toll, or that all of his love simply could no longer fit in his chest. He breathed deeply to calm himself while a cold sweat ran down his brow and the nape of his neck. After a few minutes the pain went away, but he knew that it would return, and so he hastened to start scaling, slowly, what remained of the cocoon that was dissolving and allowing him to glimpse the moon once more. Climbing up the neck, he scaled her chin and dragged himself toward the cheek of this moon that was, fortunately, little more than a baby about to be born. A gigantic baby, to be sure, but for this reason much more manageable for a diminutive mountaineer than the massif of a woman that she had been and would be once more. The poet settled himself to wait just beneath the moon's right eye, next to the tear duct. And when the eyes finally opened and saw him, Shen Xiao realized with joy that he had achieved what nobody had in all these millennia: he had surprised a being as old as time itself. Was it just his imagination, or did the moon look at him with relief upon finding that she was not alone at her rebirth? Whatever the case, she did not move, so when the pain returned, Shen was able to stretch out peacefully on the cheek of his love and lay there, never to awaken again.

THE BUTTERFLY MAN

Yesterday I died again. Today, the room looks the same as ever. The bed in its same place, only lightly disheveled because nobody actually slept there: somebody simply died in it and later resuscitated. The drapes over the windows are also the same as ever. I draw them slightly and look outside, where the pious multitudes are praying, kneeling crammed together in the park surrounding the mansion. As it has been for decades. They wait, always wait. And there is nothing I could tell them, even if I knew something. I will give them silence to belie the wisdom that I do not have.

Leaving the room, I evade the penitents that await me beyond the door. I remember how difficult it was to expel them from my bedroom. It took me years to obtain respect for my dying hours. Only after my disappearance was I able to gain it through a new clause in the contract with my church. As I pass among the believers on my way to the kitchen, they follow me with faces that have wept all night long. Now, though, they are happy, radiant at seeing me among them once more. I have to admit: they cause me such disgust that only the force of habit makes it bearable.

Which was the worst of my deaths? Definitely not the first: that was the easiest. I think of this as I begin to eat breakfast. Serving myself some milk, I spill a bit, because it is difficult for me to use my left hand. All are watching me struggle and I know that more than one of them would like to mitigate the small disaster that I have created, that they would even lick the milk from the floor if I bade them to with a single gesture. Yet it is precisely because I know how much they yearn to please me that I prefer to do everything I can myself. So I hobble to the cleaning closet through the penitents—always strangers to me—get a mop, return to the kitchen, and clean the floor.

It is breakfast time. The first hour of reflection. As I have a cup of coffee the question of which was my most difficult death drives me again to recall the exact opposite: my easiest. My first death… Meningitis, the doctors said. Fifteen years old. In all likelihood I would be cured. But I died. I recall the mortal anguish at not knowing what would occur. Today, truthfully, I miss that feeling.

The doctors tried justifying their failure to my relatives, saying that they had no idea what the bacteria was which had attacked my brain. The next day, in the funeral parlor, I revived. With nary a sign or warning. As if I had just awoken from a sleep that was not especially deep. As if it were nothing. As if it were the most normal thing, with the exception of seeing myself surrounded by flowers and by those bereaved faces that later would become so commonplace.

That first day they believed I simply had catatonia. They took me to the hospital; no sign of the inflammation of my meninges remained. The doctors wanted to keep me there, but my father resisted. Upon returning to my house, where friends and family awaited, almost everyone thought that the doctors must have made a mistake, and the majority of them poked fun at the pedantry of "medical wisdom". The most religious among them dared even to apply the term "miracle", albeit in hushed voices because they feared my father's ardent atheism. The entire day was a party. The happiness didn't last for long, however, because that night I died again. When I awoke, I found that my family had taken the precaution not to prepare me for burial, but rather had left me in my room. This time there were more of them who exclaimed "miracle" at my revival, but I also began to see other faces, with more serious expressions, especially that of my father, which betrayed their horror at the fact that the extraordinary had snuck into our lives… Or perhaps it is better to call it an extraordinary mystery: a daily death. By the fourth day, after a third death and a third resurrection, all were desperately trying to acclimate themselves to the paranormal.

There is a board over my bed with a tally written on it. Today it must read 5,232. The number of times that I have died in the last fourteen-and-a-half years. Each day the number changes. Each day what surrounds it is exactly the same.

I had to grow accustomed to my unearned celebrity. Already on the first day, upon learning of my awakening in the funeral home, two reporters from a sensationalist newspaper had come to the house but my father summarily ejected them, vituperating the pair all the while. By the second day, the national papers were already there and all my father could do was close the curtains after they camped out front. By the third day, the entire world was there—from the major international channels on down to a random journalist from an Arabic newspaper. Afterward there was no way to prevent the world from entering our home and seizing our intimacy for their own.

It all began there. I ceased to be an adolescent and became "The Man Who Dies" and later "The Butterfly Man" for my custom of dying after living for only a day… Anyway, it is time to stop thinking. The first hour of reflection has passed. I light a cigarette (I can smoke as much as I want, of course) and head to the TV room. The penitents part to let me pass, although they do not clear out of the room, but rather follow along. Some of the boldest even dare to touch my clothes despite knowing that this could get them expelled from the mansion. But they are fortunate: today I don't feel like flying into a fury. Instead, I do what I do most of the time: pretend that these hundreds of people, who rotate each day, are not here. Instead, I take the remote control, sit in the recliner, turn on the giant screen, raise the volume as high as it goes, find the stupidest channel that I can, and veg out for a few hours to forget, as much as I can, my daily life and death.

***

Twelve p.m. The second hour of reflection. I get up from the recliner, turn off the girlfriend-swapping reality show that I was watching, and turn on the speaker system. At that moment, the zealot in charge of the penitents expels them all from the entertainment room and leaves me alone. Aside from the hours of my death and the end of the afternoon, this is the only time of day when I can be alone, according to my contract with the Church of the Butterfly, so I plan to enjoy it. As always, I make an homage to my father and listen to the music that he liked best, which then became my favorite when I lost him in both life and death.

For a moment I think of putting on the *Goldberg Variations* by Bach, a sound that always soothes me. Instead, I put on a disc of Beethoven… Concerto for Violin in D Major, op. 61, a work that was received with little enthusiasm in its own time, but which is nonetheless one of my favorites. Yes, today I want Beethoven: Bach or Mozart are perfect by nature. Beethoven, in contrast, often made mistakes and not all that he wrote was even good. So when he achieved perfection it resulted from a battle with himself and this made it all the more brilliant. I think that for this reason Beethoven reconciles me somewhat with the human race. Not all are penitents, like the imbeciles who await me outside the door. Nor are all people useless like me, whose only action in life, not praiseworthy in and unto itself, is to die each night. Sometimes I think to myself as I listen to Beethoven that men who die only once are able to transcend their insignificance and justify all the air they consume until the thread of their life breaks for good. This allows me to forget my own meanness and my own powerlessness.

I have one hour to recollect and as always, I dedicate it to my father. He was the only family I had. And now I have none. My mother is an image that only lives in my dreams. She died of cancer when I was just four years old. I see her solely as a benevolent smile in the few photos that I have of the three of us together. It was my father who raised me. "Who was my father?" is a question that I still cannot answer completely. As a public employee, he was the very picture of sobriety and restraint, but I know that when he was a law student he was involved in political demonstrations which hindered him from rising more rapidly up the ladder of the bureaucracy, so that he never achieved more than a modest salary and position. I think that he also dreamed of becoming an artist one day. Perhaps it was because of this that he subjected me to books, to music, to constant stimulation as a child, and it may explain his elation when at fourteen years old I wanted to start my own rock band, although my passion only lasted three months. Yes, my father wanted me to be the best at something, it didn't matter what, merely that I was the best. The only thing that he did not expect was that all I would master in my lifetime would be the art of visiting death one day after another. And that my father would be my first victim.

Indeed the best way to describe my father is as a frustrated and sensitive man. But he reached within himself and did his absolute best to protect me when the world invaded our lives and sought to dismember me: every schmuck demanding a chunk. The doctors who wanted to run tests on me. The reporters who wanted an audience with me every instant. The hordes of religious fanatics who spoke of the miracle of my resurrection as an omen of the end times. He tried, with the small might of a common man, to repel the assault of the world. And for a time he succeeded, until he was the first brought to his knees by the emanation from my daily death. Something difficult to define, but which I call "dark matter" and which simultaneously comprises the only knowledge which death has truly brought me and that which I most want to ignore.

My father never missed my deaths. Each night he would accompany me in the trance and take my hand until my body launched its last death rattle which, unfortunately for him, was never really the last. Every night he had to watch his son die, had to experience the agony of watching me perish. And although in his mind he knew that I would return intact the next day, that he ought to conceive of my death as if it were a child's dream, something primal within him told him that every night could be the last and he had to live as if that were the case. In the deepest corner of our animal instinct, death is encoded as something definitive, perhaps the only definitive thing; and it does not matter if our experience shows us the contrary: this instinct leads us to live it as if it were inevitable. The ultimate pain, the eternal parting.

My father was a strong man: he endured for six months. Six months of insomnia and mourning for somebody who did not pass. And I cannot forgive myself for my ingratitude, although I know that there was nothing I could have done. He never missed one of my many deaths, and I missed his only one. I could not accompany the person that I have loved most in this world into the trance that I know so well. One day, upon resuscitating, immediately after that first deep inhalation which marks my return to the world of the living, as if I were a drowned man who had been administered CPR, I saw him seated in the chair with his eyes open. I realized what had occurred and cried for the first and only time since I have started dying. I stayed with him in bereavement, waiting for a few days until it was inevitable that he be buried. I had hope that he had been infected with my same undying condition. But no: the only one afflicted was me. And perhaps it will always be this way.

I was alone. The government, with my father gone, seized the opportunity and acceded to the desire of the medical community to study me. Using the excuse that I was an orphan, they isolated me, although my aunt wanted to be my caretaker. What they were doing was illegal and they knew it, but they had the power, and as a result my aunt's legal battle to recover me stretched out over two years, in the midst of a scandal that masked a poorly disguised general complacency, because the entire world were asking themselves if I contained the final cure for death. Two years of needles and electrodes. To a certain extent I understand the tortures they put me through: my body is unique although I would give anything for it to be common. It does not merely contain the secret of an organism that revives itself, but also other secrets just as valuable. Each night my brain spends hours without oxygen, for which I should be a vegetable when I resuscitate. But no, my brain functions stay intact. So, in addition to the cure for death, could they not find the cure for Alzheimer's thanks to me? Or, given that I seem to be immune to any disease, because I only have the final illness, death itself, could my blood not serve to create a comprehensive antibiotic, the ultimate reinforcement for the immune system?... Well, no. As far as I know, they have failed to explain me. And, not knowing how I work, they have been unable to reproduce my conditions. They even conducted a study using a specimen of the unknown bacteria that had infected me, but that must have mutated, because although the patients got meningitis, they were either cured or they died in a more traditional way, that is, permanently. In the end, nobody could explain why my synaptic functions reactivated each morning, nor how my body was maintained without even the slightest form of decomposition despite the lack of oxygen. I know, too, that some of them wanted to dissect me since they hoped to find in an analysis of my organs the definitive answer. But more prudent voices, although not more benevolent, convinced the others to wait: perhaps the secret was in observing and continuing to study me, given that if they sacrificed me, there would be no turning back, they would have slain the greatest golden goose that science had ever known. It was better to wait, they argued, until I died for good and in the meantime continue analyzing the samples… though I still ask myself what would have happened if they would have cut me up in pieces. I have reason to be curious.

Finally, I reached the age of majority and the day of my liberation arrived. When I went out into the world, it received me as if it had missed me. Hungrily. The cameras followed me, the invitations to television programs came, the entire world wanted to take a photo with me. I began to live off my death. I made piles of money. I was very young… What would a young person want? Especially one who is rich and has been locked away for a long time? Popularity, friends, and women, no? I had popularity. I was—and am—the most famous man on Earth. Yet for some reason I have been unable to maintain even a single friendship. My old friends avoided me as if they had never known me, and the "new friends", who smiled so much during the parties, were never there when I needed them. Same with the women… well, that is a particularly uncomfortable topic for me, and one which I think about only one hour per day. For now the time has come to eat lunch and later distract myself with video games for the entire afternoon. Until finally, from five to six, I have the relief of my hour of masturbation.

***

It is important to have a routine. Routine guards against madness… or makes you not notice it as much.

At six p.m. I am always more relaxed. Sex is a necessity: it makes me feel less dead. While I do it, I even feel completely alive. Only sexual pleasure can scare away my thoughts of death. When I finish, however, I always find myself more depressed than before for having to do it by myself. Once I have entered the room where I watch the movies they have brought me, and have masturbated and cleaned up, I find myself again among the Butterfly's faithful. It is strange: I am not aroused by any of the penitents although I fantasize about almost every woman my age that I see on television, and in the past when I would leave this house, about almost every woman that I would meet at parties. I do not just fantasize about sex, moreover: I imagine that I have a girlfriend, that I take her by the hand in the street and we go out to get ice cream, we dance, we kiss. This, at least, I experienced once: yes, I know the taste of a kiss and I cannot forget it. Yet, though I think that she liked me when we were fourteen, intimacy with me is unappealing to anybody and she is no exception, even if she were not already married with two kids. Only my father put up with me because of his love for me, but that love subjected him to a trial so difficult that it eventually killed him. I think that for this reason I accepted the penitents' proposal. They are not my companions, but at least they will put up with my company, since they view me not as a man but rather as a god.

It all began with my aunt and the evangelical pastor. The man had just returned from missionary work in the Amazon, where he had been searching for God and finding nothing. He heard about my story when he returned and thought that he saw in me a manifestation of the divine. Like every fanatic who martyrs themselves or martyrs other people for their cause, I appeared to him as a sign shot directly from heaven to his heart. He wanted to be the Peter of my Church—in fact, he changed his name to "Peter"[*] given his ancestry—and he was obstinate in becoming so, such that during the two years that my aunt's fruitless legal battle ensued, he accompanied my aunt constantly and, in the process, brainwashed her. When I got out, my aunt insisted and insisted. What's more, she had changed: before she looked at me with affection, now she looked at me with fear; reverent fear, but fear nevertheless. She would even fall to her knees upon seeing me. For this reason, I stopped seeing her. However, after three years of parties and fame, I was fed up, and the cameras would not leave me in peace. So I returned to her. That was when I accepted the offer to become a god.

---

[*] t/n. The name the missionary adopts—"Peter"—is in English in the original Spanish text.

They already had the flag ready when I arrived. The symbol of my church. A white butterfly silhouetted with black lines on a red background. In reality the insect that they worship is not a butterfly, but the drawing is so stylized as to resemble one. It is actually a Mayfly, of the order Ephemeroptera (from the Greek *ephemeros*: "ephemeral" or "short life", and *pteron*, which means "wing"). Truthfully, a graceless dragonfly, but on the flag it even looks attractive. The mayfly lives for months as a nymph, but once it has wings, it only stays alive for anywhere from half an hour to one day, depending on the species. Perhaps for this reason it is also called "Dayfly", which suits me for obvious reasons. I have read a lot about the symbol, but the truth is that to this point I have not found anything good to say about the animal, aside from the fact that, because it is an insect of aquatic environments and very sensitive to pollution, you can safely drink the water from rivers and creeks where it is found. And clearly, it at least has one day of sex in which to reproduce. So I have to envy even a river fly.

At first I wanted to be a good god and was very attentive to the ceremonies. But I quickly grew bored and although I have not fallen asleep even once since I began dying, thanks to the sermons I began to appreciate anew the wonders of yawning. Consequently, they take it very well when I excuse myself from the services. In the contract that I signed with the Church I promised only to accept the daily intrusion of two hundred penitents chosen for their zeal or for their tithes. And only for one day, since I think that neither they nor I could tolerate one another's presence for any longer. They are prohibited from touching me or talking to me. The zealots, who also rotate, are charged with enforcing this. Moreover, all of them have to be content with my "majestic silence", as affirmed by the pamphlet—translated into sixty-three languages—about this mansion whose religious name I refuse to repeat even in my head. My muteness lends me an air of dignity.

They conduct the sermon without me. And they do it in all media. My Peter's program is broadcast in most of the nations of the world and he has acquired sufficient power to topple the aspirations of political candidates in more than one country. I don't really know what they preach in my name. I resist knowing about it at all. All I know is that it has to do with the only thing which distinguishes me: with death, perhaps because Peter has not been able to forget the customs of his old preachings… All religions based more upon death than on life should be prohibited. If I can say anything with authority it is that. I don't know, maybe one day I will be inspired to become the Samson of my own Church. Or perhaps not, since I need the penitents although I despise them. They are the only ones truly able to tolerate my presence… When I reflect on this, I console myself by thinking how it may already be far too late for me to break the chain of events that has been unleashed around me.

Nevertheless, I still take comfort in the knowledge that I wasn't always a coward: I tried at least once. And I tried with the type of courage that can only be born from ultimate desperation.

But it is already time for dinner.

***

I feel my bloated belly. The dinner prepared by the chef whom I never see was good. Splendid, in fact. And I enjoyed it. Yes, I enjoy the sensation of being full. I, who was always skinny, have begun to fatten up. My body is alive. This placates me. I eat, piss, shit, breathe. There are no moments I enjoy more than those in which I feel my body. Then I don't think. Then I simply exist.

Later I grow lonely and begin to talk to myself. After all, who can I converse with? A penitent has grown annoying. He is leaning over me murmuring while I rub my stomach. He tries to kiss my feet, but a zealot detains him, hoists him from the floor and takes him away. The penitent must be somebody powerful or rich, not just very faithful, because they do not pummel him as they carry him away.

One time I couldn't take it any longer. I escaped from the mansion. I was twenty-seven years old. I absconded in disguise in the middle of the afternoon as if I were just another penitent. But in the city my own image waited to trap me and make me recall the impossibility of escape. It was, stretched to absurdity, the manifestation of the famous phrase: "Nobody can escape from himself"… Yes, I awaited myself. Me, everywhere. In announcements, in newspapers, in books, on the television. I had forgotten that this city had been converted into my own Mecca. An entire city that lived for me: I was the blood that sated all of the leeches. The city lived from the hawking of my wares and from the tourism that the mansion brought in, since many of the believers came here simply to be close to me, not being able to get into the mansion itself. Encountering so vividly the horror of Borges' mirrors served to demolish my last animal resistance to carrying out the plan I had concocted.

But first I had to do something. Making sure to cover my face well, I went into a drug store and purchased hair dye, an electric razor, and makeup. In an optician's I got some blue contact lenses. I disguised myself as well as I could and upon observing the bald man with sky-blue eyes and blonde eyebrows that looked out at me from the bathroom of the public restroom, I was surprised. This wasn't me. And the image filled me with relief. I was virtually unrecognizable, and the nascent night would take care of the rest. Then I went in search of the heart of the city, where misery reigned and dirty money rushed through the alleys in torrents.

I found the brothel by its red light, and entered. There, I sought out the least attractive woman. She was old and worn down by her job. I was even scared that she would not be able to get me hard. But I had gone there with only one purpose: lose my virginity before proceeding with my real plan. So I sought her out and, after agreeing on a price, I took her to a room. She undressed and I undressed. It was somewhat frightening to look at her and her odor made me retch. But I wanted to know… and I found out. When she bent down to stimulate me, something within her changed. It was as if she had seen me for the first time, as if she had smelled me and realized what everyone who knows me was already aware of. She began to tremble and then excused herself, saying that she didn't feel well. I stayed alone in the room, feeling the weight of my burden and of my eternal solitude.

Dark matter… that's what I call it. There is something missing in the universe: if the star systems that we see were all that existed, the universe would have a completely different form than the one it currently has. In astronomy, dark matter is the missing mass that makes the equations square and maintains the current equilibrium of the cosmos. That which we do not see, but which we know exists. Which is why I also apply this term to the negative charge that has installed itself in me because of my quotidian encounter with death, and which everyone else perceives almost as soon as they come near me, even though they are not conscious of it. It is as real as a fragrance, but harder to define. And all feel it. What's more, unlike a butcher or an executioner, I cannot wash the blood of the day off me because it is my own blood. For this reason, people cannot bear my contact for very long… What does it alert them to about themselves? The certainty that one day they will die? The unbearable weight of their precious lives and how they squander them every day?… I don't know. All I know is that not even a prostitute, accustomed to receiving all the despicable dregs of the earth, could suffer my emanation, and that I was alive only until I was fifteen years old: ever since then I have existed, but I have not lived. The redemption of Eros has been denied to me: I belong entirely to Thanatos, whether I like it or not. I have done nothing more than die, and I do not really enjoy anything. Therefore I know too well that existence is worthless without Eros, if it is not based in pleasure and in creation. A religion does not merit the name if it is centered on a cult of death, if above all else it tries to diminish the terror of disappearing instead of encouraging the enjoyment of the days that we live in this world. It was for this reason that I wanted to destroy my Church. And if one day I find a new way to do so, perhaps I will be energized to try again… Or perhaps I will always be terrified by the outcome of my first attempt.

The story of what happened next is simple. I went directly from the brothel to the mansion. There, the entire world was looking for me. The news of my disappearance had already gone global. The cameras and the multitudes thronged the grounds. I slowly pushed toward the security cordon and there, somebody recognized me. The way opened up immediately and the cameras focused on me, so they witnessed me approach the nearest policeman. I don't know why the man did not react to what I did, perhaps because he was a believer or simply because seeing me in person intimidated him, but regardless he did not try and prevent me from taking the pistol that he had holstered on his belt. With the gun in hand, nothing could stop me: I took off the safety, put the barrel in my mouth, feeling the cold muzzle against my palate, pulled the trigger without even flinching, and the bullet shot straight through my brain.

But it is already time that I prepare myself to die again.

***

While I lay in bed I miss reading. A couple of years ago I always enjoyed reading at this time of night, before the tremors would begin. I had even come to envy characters in the works of Dostoevsky and Sartre. Perhaps it is true that the lives television shows me hurt me less, since they cause me less envy; they are insipid, insubstantial, hollow, almost as meaningless as my own. But in truth I miss reading.

It is 8:55 p.m. Within an hour and a half, I will die. At 10:22 p.m. exactly. Always at the same time, with the exception of the day that I committed suicide. That day I died at 8:08 p.m. But not only did I fail that day, I also paid a steep price for the defeat. Although the next morning I resuscitated at the same time as always—6:48 am—I did not return intact. The bullet wound closed that night while I was dead, but the affected brain tissue was not replaced; it simply scarred over. As a result, I am incapable of reading now because I suffer from profound dyslexia, I limp when I walk, I cannot speak intelligibly, I have a tic in my left eye, and my left hand trembles beneath the slightest burden.

I cannot kill myself. And now I know quite well, as I am the only one who can speak to this point from practice and not just in theory, that every person should at least have the possibility of electing to die. That choice, even if we do not use it, guarantees that we can preserve a modicum of dignity in impossible circumstances. I do not have it… I am lowlier than everyone else.

Perhaps I chose the wrong method. Perhaps it was something as stupid as the horror movies I had seen which brought me to put a bullet in my brain. In those films, that was the only method to put an end to what I have become: a living corpse. Yet I am terrified at what would have happened if I had committed suicide by other means: decapitating myself, for example. Or breaking my neck while hanging myself. I would continue existing, but without a body. And if I had made an even more radical decision, like setting myself on fire, who could guarantee that my consciousness would not linger in the form of particles? And who could even give me a notion of how horrible that would be?... To be everywhere without remaining anywhere.

Old age also scares me for this reason. I am deteriorating. I know it. Perhaps I will never die, though. Not even when I no longer have the least control over my body and my mind has ceased to possess any notion of myself. I will putrefy without dying. My only hope is that one day they will discover a weapon so powerful that it can dissolve even an atom and its memory. A weapon of dark matter. A weapon of total negation... Yes, I will wait until that weapon appears or my body threatens to deny me the least autonomy if I wait for even one more day, because the worst part about my failure was not what occurred with my brain, but rather that it achieved the opposite effect of what I had hoped: instead of destroying that monster which was born from my death, I strengthened it.

The church said that my sacrifice had been to convince the skeptics. Every human being on the planet saw my brains fly out on camera. Then they saw me alive the next day. Now there are more believers than ever. And I do not have a voice to explain the true intent of my actions.

***

It is 9:58 p.m. I will lose consciousness shortly. I am completely covered in cold sweat. My pulse is quickened. My chest seems to break with the heaving effort of each breath. It hurts. It hurts so much.

The best-kept secret of my Church is that dying is anguish for their god. Dying is not simply unpleasant; it is terrible. There is no way to become accustomed to it. My body resents that reality, everything in me cries out for mercy. It is irrelevant that I know I will keep on living. My body suffers. My body howls. I believe that for this reason the Church has never permitted me to be seen in my moment of transition. A very different story than what happened with my other bit of privacy, to be alone during the hours I am dead, which I had to win through many battles after my suicide, expelling from my room with enraged gestures the penitents who were there every morning upon my resurrection.

My body suffers so much that I must already be in hell. Perhaps it is so. Perhaps my first was my only true death and everything else has been a punishment for offenses that I no longer recall. Yes, perhaps all of this is the hallucination of a body already dead. Or maybe this is my soul's punishment, that hell consists of existing forever without the ability to die.

But I know all too well that it is not so. I know quite well that my deaths are real. That the pain and the solitude are real.

Death is the ultimate lover.

Every night I dream that she embraces me for a few hours.

And every day I awake only to discover that she has rejected me once more.

THE ESSENCE OF THE JOURNEY

The newborn had only three legs. Inside the cave, those invited to witness the birth of the new centaur kept quiet in an attempt to respect the pain of the parents, but whinnies of distress escaped a few of them and the echo against the stone walls amplified the volume, which provoked nervous snorts from the others in attendance.

The baby was, in all other respects, a handsome exemplar of a centaur, as everybody had expected a child of his parents would be. Yet his physical defect could not have been more notable. He was missing his entire front right leg. The way in which this would handicap him for the rest of his life was undeniable from the moment when, as soon as he was free from the placenta, following his instincts he tried to rise and reach his mother's nipples, only to fall to the ground time and time again. He did not cry from the impacts and cast aside his encumbrance in order to try again, without giving up. But he failed. A failure that meant death, because if he could not even stay standing long enough to drink milk, he would be even less capable of keeping pace with his race of nomads the next day, since custom dictated that the pause in migration for a new birth last only one day.

Nobody stated the obvious. If centaurs were in no way a race of whiners, they were even less a race of charlatans. Even in that primitive era they had already internalized the most elemental form of courtesy: if you aren't going to say something useful, it is better to say nothing at all. For this reason, a few minutes after the tragedy was completely evident, those invited vacated the cave making as little noise as possible.

Once they were alone, his parents finally looked one another in the eye. Red-Loin, the male, felt guilty at his inability to identify the emotion that had led him to avert his eyes from his wife until that moment. Somebody more experienced with dread would have known that it was fear, pure and simple: the dread of knowing her decision regarding the problem that they both faced. And his nightmare came true, because he read in Breathe-Deep's eyes what he already suspected: she would not consent to abandon her young or to give him a miserable death as tradition dictated for lost causes. She would stay and he would lose her, since before being a father or a husband, his foremost duty was to keep guiding the herd as its most experienced hunter, and if he stayed, not only would he dishonor himself, he would also make her into a pariah for having dragged him away from his duty. Both were cognizant of it: it was tradition, it was custom. And custom, everybody knew, was there to guarantee the survival of the herd in a hostile world.

Red-Loin loved his wife. He lowered his eyes, then, and left the cave, practically dragging his hooves but without saying a word. Breathe-Deep loved her husband and, upon seeing him leave, did her name justice by inhaling intensely and then with hands still trembling from the effort of giving birth and from the pain of parting, offered her child sufficient support so that limping on his three legs he could approach the wall and leaning against it drink from her nipple, shakily, before laying down on the ground and going to sleep, exhausted.

The next morning the herd left.

***

Apart from the fact that, thanks to his mother he survived when he should have died, there is not much to be said about the childhood of the lame centaur. Nevertheless, what little there is to relate is key: first and foremost, he learned to walk. His balance improved, growing accustomed to supporting the bulk of his weight always on his hind legs, such that when he moved he only had to hold himself fleetingly over his single front leg. Perhaps it would never be a graceful motion, but it worked, and although he never could reach the average speed of a centaur or keep running for very long before his legs began to flag, it was sufficient to allow him to become a hunter, like all of his race. He was especially effective in the forest, where the tree branches allowed him to use his arms to support part of his weight, and with the bow, since his arrow shafts had the speed that his flesh lacked.

Given that he had no socialization aside from conversations with his mother before bed or upon waking, where she taught him everything she knew, he focused on learning every-thing about the forest of that valley that they both inhabited, until he could recognize every rock, every branch, every flower. He learned to distinguish the different tracks that the myriad animals left on the ground, in the air, or in their scent, and to discern other traces in the color of broken branches or in the structure of dung, thanks to which he was able to become a great tracker.

Nothing, however, prepared him for the encounter that he had at age fourteen. That day he was returning from the hunt when he heard a great racket of hooves striking the ground near the cave. Approaching, he confirmed the evident: the centaurs had returned. The great cycle which traversed the immense steppes of Central Asia and the forests of the north had been completed and now they were returning to this little corner at the edge of Europe where he had been born. More than three hundred mouths were speaking, drinking, eating, and neighing around the creek near the cave. Timidly, the ad-olescent centaur approached the group and, when he pene-trated the semicircle formed by the herd, many eyes fell upon him, more than one surprised: the young at seeing a three-leg-ged centaur for the first time; the old, at finding him still alive. An enormous centaur stepped forward and after looking at Breathe-Deep, who hovered at the entrance to the cave, he put his arm around the young one's shoulders and guided him into the center of the herd.

So, on the arm of his father, he was integrated into the society of centaurs and received a name. According to their pragmatic tradition, he was simply called Three-Legs. That night he reclined in front of the bonfire and listened to the stories of the hunters, wherein they brought his mother up to date on what was taking place in the world, principally those things related to wild boars and the herds of aurochs, giant wild cattle which were the favorite prey of the centaurs because they were the most worthy in combat. They also told her of the advance of their greatest enemies, humans, who in recent times seemed unstoppable, spreading like a plague over all of their hunting grounds. In the last clash between the species, two seasoned hunters had died, Green-Eye and Silent-Run, and although more than a score of human hunters had perished as well, the loss had been greater for the centaurs, since their numbers were already greatly reduced and, as nomadic tribes, they needed vast swaths of territory to hunt. As far as they knew, there were only three other herds, one on each of the continents, while humans founded a new settlement practically every day. Nevertheless, the conversations began to diminish since centaurs grew tired of talking and instead preferred to sink into silence for long stretches in order to enjoy their preferred sounds: the rumor of the air moving in the forest, the distant sound of a stream, the deliberate respiration of plants, and the whisper of the insects within the grass.

The next day, the herd began its march again, enlarged by the two members that it had once left behind. But just a few hours later it was evident that the adolescent would not be able to maintain the pace. Although he did not complain, because he knew what failure meant here, his hooves hurt him so badly that he thought they would crack, his heartbeat heaved as furiously as a bellows gone wild, and his mouth began to spew foam specked with spots of blood. It was obvious that his fight was in vain and the herd came to a halt. Breathe-Deep walked up to her son, embraced him, looked at him with pride and sadness, placed her forehead against his and, after shedding a single tear, returned to the head of the herd and began the march again beside her husband.

For a long time, the adolescent did not move. Later, when night had already begun to fall, he slowly returned to the valley where he was born. The next morning he arrived at the cave, but he did not want to enter, because he had just realized that returning had been pointless: nothing awaited him there. Then the instinct of his race arose like a breeze within his head, a surging wind, because for so long that message whispering in his mind had been kept quiet. Now, it impelled him to travel, to move, to go far away. So he set off in the opposite direction from the herd. He went south. Alone.

***

When he came to the sea some weeks later his legs hurt him like never before. Furthermore, he discovered that the sound of the ocean soothed him, so he decided to establish himself there. It was the beginning of several years of solitude. Perhaps a man would have been driven mad, but Three-Legs was not a man. As a centaur, everything in him was hardened, built to survive. So, instead of lamenting his solitude, he decided to always keep himself busy. His first challenge was to improve his abilities as a hunter and, given that he could not run fast enough to overtake his prey, he had to resort to cunning. In spite of his limp, he learned to move so stealthily that the animals he ate never heard him until he was close enough to fell them with his bow, whose arrows always flew true. But a centaur does not live by the hunt alone. Since he belonged to a nomadic and gregarious people, he had to solve two great puzzles: how to find somebody to talk to and how to travel without moving.

The first problem was easy to solve. He decided to tell himself stories and to create memories which he could talk to himself about. Although he did not have a name for his crazy idea, he resolved to draw pictures in the caverns where he lived to remind him of his hunts, of his mother, and of the world that he had known. That way, when he saw the drawings, he would be able to converse with himself and avoid going crazy from lack of company.

Harder to settle was his instinct to travel. It took him years to find a solution. At first he was limited to recalling what his mother had told him of the great steppes to the east of the enormous northern forests, and also what he had heard during the only night in which he had accompanied the herd. Yet his need to travel begged more from him than memories. He wanted to see the sites to which his mind traveled. So he decided to paint with his colorful imagination the places that he had never been. But this also quickly became insufficient. He began then to dream up journeys which took him far, far away, further than his people had ever gone. He complemented with fantasy what little he had heard of these places, and came to know the golden deserts of Asia and the dense jungles of Africa. Upon discovering that the mind was such a good vehicle for travel his hunger, instead of being sated, intensified. So, one day, he decided to cross the ocean in the ship of his imagination, manifesting the lands beyond and—when this also proved unsatisfying—he even visited the moon.

Nevertheless, a moment arrived when he realized that he had grown so fond of his many journeys that he wanted to relive them, to carry them out. His imagination allowed him to return as many times as he wanted, but there had to be some way that each excursion could add to the sensation of reality of the one before, a way in which his travels could be smelled, tasted, seen. Words were his only path, but how could he make words permanent? This question became an obsession to which he had no answer for many years.

Meanwhile, his restless mind was dedicated to improving his living quarters and shaping his environment. His brain, which was honed by his struggle for sanity and which constituted his only vehicle for travel, stayed in a state of perpetual disquiet. He decided to ease his imprisonment by filling his den with useful objects, constructed from his preferred material: wood. At first he was satisfied by a stump retrieved from the beach on which he could eat without bending over, or a branch to hang up his quiver. But when this became insufficient, he decided to use the same knowledge that he had employed to construct his bow and arrows to enhance his dwelling, and soon his hands acquired such facility with woodworking that it seemed as if he were molding clay. In this way, uniting wood with the skins of the animals he hunted, he quickly had as comfortable a lifestyle as he could have wished, even creating furnishings which until that moment had never been seen in the world.

But his greatest area of expertise arose from the simple necessity of surviving without anybody to take care of him. His people had extensive knowledge of the power of plants and every single bit of this learning had been transmitted to him by his mother. In his more than fifty years of solitude, though, he carried it even further. Beginning with the countless wounds from hunting that he had to heal and the numerous physical aches that he had to ease, he learned as no one had before the secret universe of medicine hidden within plants. What's more, the tireless curiosity that kept him sane also led him to explore the cadavers of animals in order to understand the functions of his own body. He learned much this way. So much indeed, that one day it was this learning which brought his solitude to an end.

He was hunting in the hills, like any other day, when he found himself face to face with one of the few lions that remained north of the Mediterranean. Three-Legs observed the prey that the lion was dragging, watching it wriggle while the predator's mandibles held it securely in place, its feeble struggle hardly bothering the hunter at all. The centaur thought for a moment of leaving and allowing nature to take its course, but he had not seen a face similar to his own in so long. Besides, the human cub that the lion held, although it belonged to another species, reminded him of his own.

The lion was old; if it had not been, it would not have risked hunting a human; incapable of chasing after more agile yet inoffensive prey. Seeing the centaur approach, he dropped his catch on the ground and let out a roar. However, when he saw the centaur nock an arrow, the world-weary lion knew that he had lost the battle and decided to withdraw. With bitterness he reflected that no matter whether it was centaurs or humans, this territory belonged to them now and was his no longer. Furious but powerless, he backed away, still roaring and glaring at the centaur to cover his wounded pride. Finally, he turned around and marched off to find other quarry with which to satisfy his hunger.

The centaur continued looking at the child. The torso, similar to his own from the waist up, was shredded open and blood flowed profusely from the wounds. However, he was still writhing and weakly moaning. Placing his bow on his back, Three-Legs picked the child up in his arms and returned to his cave. There he placed him on the table that he had constructed from a dead tree and some boar skins, and for four days and nights fought against death with all that he knew and all the strength he could muster.

When the child of around eight years regained consciousness, the first thing that he did was look at Three-Legs in terror. But the centaur mollified him by giving him something to eat and drink without even trying to speak to him, since the little one's language was very different from that of the centaur. Afterward, as the child ate, Three-Legs pondered what to do with him. Where did he come from? How had he gotten there? This was his most immediate concern. As a result, once the boy had eaten, Three-Legs covered him with a blanket and left to go and explore. He came to the place where he had encountered the lion with his prey, and followed the trail that the boy's body had left as it was dragged. A little ways away he saw smoke and, from a hill where he could see without being seen, he studied the village. It was a new human settlement, which, as the hunters had told him decades ago, were being constructed in so many places by this species that was laying claim to the world. The houses of the centaurs' most lethal adversaries were still half-built. The building materials of straw, clay, and sand were still being integrated into the constructions, such that they appeared to be strangers forced to live together who did not trust one another, insufficient time having passed for them to bond like a group that knew each other well. The fires of the forges in particular drew his attention, since centaurs were not familiar with metal, only with wood and stone. Finally, after observing for more than half an hour, he made up his mind.

At dawn he brought the child in his arms and, eluding the sentinels thanks to the darkness, deposited him near the bonfire, leaving him dressed in a deerskin. Then he fled with all the velocity his three legs could bear and, once in his cave, began preparing defenses, constructing a wall, and whittling his arrows, in case the humans came looking for him.

But the humans did not come. At least not for three months. And when they finally did, they did not arrive with intent to attack. Ten men presented themselves in broad daylight. They left their weapons outside the wall, where the centaur could see them. They had brought four children with them—half of the children in the hamlet—poisoned from drinking contaminated water. They burned with fever and were dehydrated from diarrhea. Three-Legs looked at them indecisively... It was clear what they wanted, knowing what he had done with the wounds from the previous child, and the centaur intuited that it had not been easy for them to decide to bring the children. "What to do?" thought Three-Legs. Accepting them meant having relations with humans and he was unsure whether this would end poorly. But ultimately he elected to try healing the kids and for several days he attended to them. The men stayed beyond the wall this entire time, although they left provisions for him just outside. When the children were cured, the centaur bid them goodbye and thought that that would be the last of it.

However, the humans needed him more than he needed them. Accidents were frequent and illness was a constant companion in the village. For a community so small, each death was a tragedy, so they grew accustomed to turning to the centaur every time that they had need of him. In exchange for his care they always left him provisions.

In his contact with his patients, the centaur learned the human language. It was not easy, since it was full of abstract concepts, very removed from the daily reality of a wild being. And perhaps for a nomadic centaur it would have been impossible. But it was not for Three-Legs, since he, in his prolonged solitude, had become accustomed to reflecting on things for which he did not even have concepts, like the sensation that intoxicated him each time he saw the sea in the morning, or the distant lands that he could see in his imagination. Beyond this he had plenty of time for thought, since his life would last several times as long as that of a man. In fact, with respect to certain experiences or reflections that the humans shared with him, Three-Legs felt that he had already explored those ideas much further than they had, even if up until that moment he had lacked the language to describe what the people expressed to him.

With the passing decades, the relationship between the centaur and the humans was cemented. Soon the small community, always on the verge of being swept away, began to rely so heavily on him that they consulted him about other problems besides medicine. Thus, the day came when, facing a drought that threatened to spoil the harvest, the humans asked him to visit the fields that had been sown. Already accustomed to his neighbors' petitions, the centaur assented and, with the pragmatism of his species and his own natural curiosity, he spent a few hours analyzing the problem before proposing to the humans a solution so simple that they kicked themselves for failing to see it before; taking advantage of their construction skills, they should bring water from a nearby creek by carving furrows in the earth. That night, as thanks, they invited him to a party in the village, where the women placed a crown of grape leaves on his forehead and gave him a drink to try which left him dizzy. Without knowing why, he began to chuckle, and laughed even harder when he found out that his neighbors had started to think of him as something of a god, that concept being so incomprehensible for a centaur, the most practical of all those that humans call fantastical beings.

The relationship between the centaur and the humans was unshakable from that point forward. Thanks to the counsel of Three-Legs, the village began to grow until it reached the size of a city in keeping with the standards of the age; three hundred total inhabitants who, before the death of the centaur two hundred-fifty years later, would become more than three thousand, since immigrants began to arrive, aware of the prosperity of the place.

The centaur was nourished by the anxieties of the humans; he was thankful for the challenges that their survival put to his wandering mind and there was no science into which he did not desire to foray. As for the human beings, whose spark had been lost due to their sedentary lifestyle, they were nourished by the anxieties of that mental nomad. For example, Three-Legs, intrigued by the mystery of the metals unknown to his species, asked them to explain to him the secrets of the bronze forge. Later he began to experiment with other metals and constructed ovens that were larger each time, arriving at the discovery of how to work with one of the most abundant materials. But just as he had explained the technique of iron-working to the humans, he abandoned his interest in metallurgy and concentrated on teaching.

His relationship with the children of the village was especially robust. Their presence eased the emptiness that arose from a powerful, insatiable instinct, since he knew quite well that he would never have children of his own. So, once he had passed so much time with the villagers that the boy he had rescued from the lion had already died of old age, he proposed to the men and women of the city which he had helped raise that they cede their children to him each morning so that he could teach them everything he knew. The parents assented and this was how the first school was born.

Three-Legs, who by now the humans knew by another name in their own language, dedicated himself to teaching the arts of the hunt, of medicine, of the forge, of artisanry. He discovered that he had found his true passion. The school began to swell and its fame spread as widely as that of the nascent city beside it. Soon other metropolises began to send their children to learn with the centaur. Each time more travelers came to meet him, all carrying stories and knowledge from towns and cities far away.

So many tales brought so much knowledge that increasingly the centaur felt the urgency of his long unresolved question: how to travel without moving and, nevertheless, conserve in reality what one has seen and felt with one's imagination. He pondered this night upon night after his grueling teaching shifts, until one day, looking at the impression that a branch tugged by the tide left in the sand, he had an idea. Why not draw sounds? Why not give a solid form to the air? He retrieved a stick and tried to draw in the sand the sound of the sea. Afterward he looked at the sign that he had made and realized that this was only the beginning.

He spent many years perfecting his idea, tailoring the symbols, listening closely to the distinct sounds in order to give them a precise form, breaking them apart to unite them once more. Meanwhile, he continued teaching. Children came and went, until he judged that his final and most wonderful invention was ready to be imparted. So he called in his two favorite students: a swift-footed blonde boy who reminded him of his own constant disquiet, and a blind brunette boy who, like himself, should have been sacrificed at birth but instead had survived. And he began to slowly explain to them the marvels of his invention.

As the three of them sat together on that morning when the teacher began to instruct his students how to draw symbols in the sand, using a branch to give words a body more solid than the air, none of them suspected the influence that the new invention would have on their lives or on the world. Not the blonde boy, whose deeds, life, and death would be indelibly marked in memory thanks to the signs that he was then learning to combine. Nor the blind boy, who would be the first and the greatest of all the poets. Nor he whom the humans knew as Chiron, the Centaur, who should not have lived, but instead survived to found a civilization.

THE SERPENTS AWAKEN

I ask myself when she will arrive. It is cold… only I remain. All of the others have fled. They abandoned the blind in the place where he belongs: behind. I do not know this house and, in my condition, to be in an unfamiliar place is almost the same as being on another planet. If I get up and try to find the bathroom, especially when I am so terrified, there is no certainty that I would be able to return to the mattress where I presently abide. I could count my steps incorrectly, mistake some corner for another, and become lost in the desert of this abandoned city. So I would rather hold it in as long as I can and wait here, without moving.

Yes, it is very cold, although in this city nestled between temperate seas, it should be scorching summer. But I think that it is mostly loneliness and fear that make me huddle up in this blanket. And an idle question unravels itself as I worry the fabric; a question that distracts me from this nightmare that will conclude, inevitably, with my own end: What color is the blanket covering me?… A futile inquiry, as unanswerable for me as whether or not God cares about the fate of humanity. Although, now that He has abandoned us all, the question seems to answer itself. Yet it is better to think of the colors that I cannot see to occupy the time that I have left rather than the other option I have in my abandonment: asking myself how I will die. How she will kill me. I know that if I could see her, the sight alone would finish me. There is no certainty about what happens to the blind, though. Nobody can attest to it, since the only thing certain is that there are no survivors. The sighted or the blind.

Eleven years have passed since she arrived. And she leaves death everywhere she walks. Every city through which she passes transforms into a wasteland. Into a void replete with buildings, where nothing will grow again, so saturated with radiation that its reclamation is impossible. It does not matter which metric you use, she is the end.

Is anybody left in Europe besides me? The cradle of scientific civilization is empty. Europe lies in ruins once more, although this time not a single building has fallen. It is the ultimate ruin: the absence of humanity. All have fled… but where have they gone? England showed that not even islands are secure. How did she get there? Walking beneath the water? Can she survive without oxygen? These questions summarize everything that we truly know about her nature: nothing. What we do know is that she has changed the world more radically than any human conqueror or thinker. That same world that once seemed to us so secure, so predictable. A world that only we humans had the right to disorder with our games of ambition… But after ten thousand years of living in cites, it has taken little more than a decade for all of the glory of Europe to sink into an irrecoverable past and for the other continents to become refugee camps. At least, those that are still standing, since Africa is also a ruin, but this was done in the traditional manner: at the hands of man. The Europeans started the war when they sought to escape south and it was their turn to find the gates shut. China is a rampart. North America accepted millions, perhaps out of fear that the Atlantic would ultimately prove no better a defense than the English Channel, and when their turn came, they would find nobody who would receive them. I was in New York when, after finishing with Spain, the curse wheeled back toward the east instead of crossing the ocean; I still remember the celebrations of relief at seeing the end postponed. The South Americans hawked their ample lands as if they were covered in diamonds, reclaiming the gold upon which Europe had erected its power in recent centuries: another cycle that was fulfilled. Only Australia has kept its doors firmly shut, confident in being the last fortress of the species that will fall… It may even be that the Aussies are delusional enough to think that it will take her more than a lifetime to get to them.

When she first appeared and cleared out Rome, the initial theory was that she was a new virus. One which caused death instantaneously. A virus does not spread at the pace of a person walking, however. Nor does it cross through hazmat suits, like the ones worn by those who went to verify what happened to the cities with which all communication had been lost. First Italians, then Swiss, Germans, Scandinavians, Dutch, French, and many more since then. She advances slowly. Inexorably.

For this reason the quarantine has not been effective. It is futile to block off the airports and close the borders when death simply walks. Soldiers stay at attention in their posts, communicating with their superiors and ready to enter the fray, until the moment that she comes close. Then they die. And nothing but silence remains.

The scientists who pronounced the new virus were quickly replaced by the believers. They proclaimed that her name was Plague, one of the four riders of the Apocalypse, and as proof argued that it was no coincidence that she had begun her march in the City of Saint Peter. Even today the churches are still packed, but there are many more of us who now believe that an old curse, long dormant, has been resurrected. Especially after listening in terror to the flight of that aviator who offered themself to fly over the disaster zone and announce what it was that threatened the species. And those unforgettable words that they pronounced before their glider crashed and which summarize all that we ultimately know about who will kill us: "A woman… around her, serpents. It hurts to look at her… Unbearable."

Twelve words encapsulate all of our species' knowledge on the most important subject. Of course, there has been no shortage of volunteers to try and learn more, but all have proved useless. Just as ineffective have been the unmanned probes, which have failed a thousand times. Proximity to her seems to affect every electronic instrument the same way that a nuclear blast would. Our satellites, despite their distance, burn up when they try to focus on her with their cameras. Even for the inanimate her gaze spells doom. The name with which she was finally baptized suits her well: the Gorgon. There were in total three Gorgons of Greek myth, all sisters. Medusa is the best known, punished by Athena for having been raped by Poseidon in his temple by being transformed into a monster with serpents for hair, who turns to stone anybody that looks upon her. The return of the myth has ended the dominion of science over the world.

How many times have we tried to kill her? First, with well-qualified assassins who never returned. Next, with high tech toys that malfunctioned before they could reach her: the missiles crashed too early, the jets plummeted from the sky, the explosives blew up in the bomb bays of the gliders. Finally, the time came for biological and chemical weapons which awaited her arrival before expelling their contents. But the few times that these did not disarm themselves before exploding, all that we achieved was doubling the toxicity of the air in the abandoned cities. I wonder how desolate Hagia Sofia and the Blue Mosque must appear, just a couple of kilometers from where I wait. What to do with a church or a mosque that no longer has the hope of receiving believers who recall the floor mosaics and azulejos with which they are consecrated? It would have been more merciful to bomb them than to let them suffer the humiliation of a caller capable of expelling God as if he were a leper.

Which leads me, the only inhabitant of Istanbul, to ask myself where the stalking doom will elect to go next: Asia or what remains of Africa? This city is the crossroads. She has to pass through here. Which will fall first? On whom will she settle after finishing off the center of Christianity? Will she go toward the Muslim countries, or the Buddhist ones? Does she even care? For her all religions must be the same.

It grows colder. The silence is total. When I lost my vision, I was elated to find that what I had heard was true: the other senses are sharpened when one loses that which constitutes our species' principal sense. But today I am doubly blind… at first I tried to clap or shout, but the echo in an empty city is so terrifying that silence quickly became comforting. So I resigned myself to accepting that all of my senses are blind. All except for touch, which transmits this glacial cold to me. Is it true that we are in summer or have I been fooled?… Upon arrival I was even prepared to smell the odors that my imagination had associated with an abandoned city: decomposing food, uncollected garbage. I was mistaken, though: there are few odors, because nobody remains to produce them, humans or animals, and theirs was not a hasty flight. It was an orderly evacuation, planned with months of notice. It is the only advantage that her slowness gives us. Nevertheless, it is an advantage in appearance only. We are like cockroaches which an exterminator drives from the nest and which take refuge in the next hiding place. When all of the survivors of the species are heaped one atop another in the last refuge, she will sweep us all away. It could take decades, but there is only one possible outcome: total extermination… I wonder if she enjoys it: if so, if she is a cruel killer and not just cold-blooded, perhaps the best analogy is not of exterminators and cockroaches, but rather of a bullring, where all of humanity is the animal and she is the matador. There is an illusion of combat, but her advantage is so great that we have no true chance of victory. For now, she is simply playing with us: we charge hopelessly. And when she wearies of the sport, she will deliver the final blow.

She draws near. I can feel it in the silence. The silence of an abandoned city is total, but this… It seems as if the air itself has ceased circulating. Even so, I feel fine. No symptoms until now of any illness. Nothing that yet proves that I have been marked by her contact. But I know that I have been: there is no way to survive having been so close. If I move away, like so many others who did not wait long enough to see her and die immediately, but did not hurry enough to avoid being tainted, mortal illness would be her apparition. "What would happen to me? How would I ultimately die?" I ask myself… Because there is not just one way to die. The Gorgon simply hastens the inevitable. Immune defenses topple before her breath and then it is revealed, approaching with giant steps, the rot aestivating within each one of us. The most fortunate die of diabetes or a stroke thirty or forty years before their time. Others develop heart defects or osteoporosis. The rest, tumors. In her presence, the genes which carry predisposition to illness mutate and the cells proliferate as if they were flowers which had just received fertilizer. Many of the refugee camps are one giant hospital, replete with bodies decomposing alive and with no hope of survival. Once you have been close to her, you can flee but you cannot escape. I will not flee… though not out of courage: simply because it is too late for that. And I am blind.

I hear footsteps, and a constant crescendoing rustle, like that of a sea which instead of water contains wet grass… I concentrate on distinguishing the weight of the steps, and I am surprised to discover that they are heavier than I expected. The cold has become a solid wall; the air itself is so dense that it seems as if I have to break through it to breathe. My lungs burn with the effort. I swaddle my body in the blanket and, stupidly, try to cover even my head. I seem like a child; I do not recognize the me that I remember. But this does not stop my body from trembling. And I know that it is not just from the cold.

The footsteps come close and stop. I strain to catch some odor, but I do not smell anything… Or do I? Is there not a very tenuous trace, almost imperceptible? Something so faint that perhaps I would not smell it if I could still see. But then I would lose the image which this aroma calls to mind: dead flowers. In a florist. One where, if you brought your nose close, you would swear that you could smell water, stagnant but not putrid: water which has not been changed in a long time.

Hidden beneath the fabric I sense the sound of movement in the room. Somebody pulls down the blanket that I am grasping as if it were an actual wall that could protect me rather than a bolt of cloth that rationally I know to be fragile. The one who forces my discovery does so firmly in order to overcome my resistance, but not violently. And when the blanket reveals my face, a hand caresses my cheek and arranges my bangs. The contact is warmer than I expected and it almost relieves me in the frigid air, but there is an unctuous quality to the palm, as if it were drenched in oil. Finally, when she is done caressing me, she takes me by the shoulders with both hands and tries to put me on my feet. By the angle at which her arms take hold of me, I discern that she is taller than I am. At first, my legs do not respond and I feel stiffness in my joints from all the time I spent huddled up, but finally I am able to hold myself upright.

When the blood flows regularly in my legs and I am left with only the nausea of terror, I sense that a hand is searching for mine. And when it makes contact, I am profoundly surprised to discover something for which the caresses on my face could not have prepared me. It is a man's hand which takes mine. Without a doubt. There is no way I am wrong about this. And an enormous relief swells in me… but the sensation lasts less than the blink of an eye, since I am immediately aware of the hissing, the rasping sound emitted by the eddy of bodies coming from where my companion's head should be. No, it is not another like me that has been left behind… Once again we were mistaken even about what little we thought we knew regarding the one who carries the promise of our species' doom. We were mistaken about everything important.

Then another form of relief comes to me. One that arises from absolute hopelessness. I know now that whatever I do, I am already dead. It is only a matter of time before the symptoms manifest themselves. But I lose none of that time thinking about how I will die. Instead I resign myself to my fate. And I accompany her, or accompany him, where their hand guides me. Leaving the house, I feel the grass moving. The hissing drowns out the stillness of everything else. It is not very loud, but it is deafening in a setting of universal silence, like a symphony brushing against the rocks, against the concrete, against what man has abandoned in his flight.

I wonder where they intend to direct me. But not much time passes before I find out. I feel the sun. Inside of the clouds that accompany our matador, always and wherever they go, there is a clearing where the light filters in. And my companion wants me to feel it. I perceive a sigh: their sigh. And when I am warmed by the sun, I also feel relieved. I relish the rays that shine on my face. They relieve me. A pair of tears roll down my right cheek… then I recall clearly who I am. And why I accepted the loss of my eyes.

My hand grabs blindly for the dagger hidden in my belt behind my back. Although it is a much-practiced movement, I do it clumsily, but he does not move, nor does he seem disturbed when I finally remove it, nor does he try to flee or to attack me. He does not even resist when my other hand takes him by the neck, feeling at the back the damp rubber of the serpents of his hair. I bring the point to his throat and feel how it sinks with little resistance into the flesh. When he falls, I lose the dagger. But bending over, my hand encounters the body at chest level and blindly gropes for the throat where the hilt is still buried. I take it with both hands and place all of my weight on it so that the blade digs in to the bone. Then I unearth the weapon and continue stabbing him. Over and over again. Mechanically. Finally, I return to the neck and work to separate the head from the trunk. Not an easy task while blind and armed only with a dagger, so it takes me a few minutes.

Holding the head in my left hand by the hair that no longer moves, I exhale with relief and exhaustion. In spite of everything, the final act was easier than I had anticipated. It was much more difficult to simply await his arrival. Perhaps because I encountered a man when I had expected to find a woman? I do not know… but I feel spent. Even so, foremost in my mind is the thought of escape. To flee, although I know that I am condemned. My feet do not respond, however. For a moment I think that it is simple weariness, but I notice that there is a resistance tying me to the floor. Quickly I fall upon the realization that the serpents are holding me back. They are climbing all over me, covering me like a creeping vine. They ascend my knees, my hips, accumulating one on top of the last, up my chest, up my neck. Their weight threatens to topple me, but they themselves take charge of bracing me so that I do not fall. Until finally nothing exists. The blackness envelops me. A blackness that has nothing to do with the emptiness of my sockets… And I thought that as a blind person I knew about darkness! Then I realize that I am not the first assassin to triumph and kill the Gorgon. Nor am I the first to be defeated by her. And so it is that, like cancer, the Gorgon does not invent the evil always latent in us, she simply activates it and allows it to reach its full potential… She is singular, but she can live within all.

And now, in this moment, it is me that she invades.

By means of the serpents that cover me, she reclaims my body as if I just had it on loan, as if she were drawn to something within me that had awoken and which had called upon her to reclaim it. When the snakes withdraw, the world is another. My hearing, my sense of smell, have opened up. But my skin, especially, has opened up. Covered now with scales, my skin transmits to me the reality all around with total clarity, in perfect detail: through the air I am aware of every pore in the walls, every crack in the pavers, every broken branch, every blade of grass, as if my entire being were a giant sonar. I smell the dampness and melancholy of a world weary of existing; the

exhausting erosion of each rock born from volcanoes and gla-
ciation, the rotting of every fallen tree, the weariness of every
drop of water, drained from time and time again transforming
into rain, evaporating, and falling again. I discover that the
world around me is cold, lovely, and sad. And that I am alone.
I am filled with an enormous desire to seek out another like
me. An enormous desire to walk. It does not matter where I
direct my steps, so long as I do not stop. So long as I never
stay in one location… There is so much to visit. So much to
see… since, although my sockets remain empty, I am no longer
blind.

She was him. He is me. She inhabits me. My hair writhes
and through their eyes I contemplate the world.

A QUESTION OF NO FUTURE

> *Now of the Sphinx's riddles there are in all two kinds:*
> *one concerning the nature of things, another concerning*
> *the nature of man; and in like manner there are two*
> *kinds of kingdoms offered as the reward of solving them:*
> *one over nature, and the other over man.*
>
> *Sphinx, or Science*, Francis Bacon

The floodgates open. I breathe deeply and get up from the seat. Before walking out I try to forget my position, of my relevance on the surface. Those rules only apply up there; not in a place where the ocean would crush me if great metal shells were not protecting me. Here I should prepare to mean nothing to anybody. Facing Her I am nobody… But it is not entirely certain that I will be nobody: if it were so, they would not have permitted me to come in person to the very center.

A technician receives me. Or one of Her priests. Same thing. Over the heart on their white lab coat there is the golden profile of the Sphinx, very small. It is ironic, since the logo is an idealization, something to make Her comprehensible, digestible to the human brain. After all, the center of Her power is an empty room and She Herself is little more than nothing. But She knows everything about everything, and so She is Everything… Or nearly so.

At least I hope as much.

There is no beauty in the passageway through which we walk. No adornment. I did not expect any, but even so it is surprising. It is part of the contrast with the world where life still subsists. A god that never errs must be impersonal, I imagine. And every thing that is here has a function. Each strip of metal, each piece of plastic, each chunk of flesh, wrapped in a lab coat, hurrying to and fro, ensuring that the Sphinx receives Her nourishment. There will be hundreds of the latter in the great hall. But before entering there, I have to pass the exam.

The technician that guided me to the first floodgate withdraws. The doors of armored glass seal hermetically, closing me in: I cannot advance to the hall, but neither can I retreat to the submarines. Ahead, separated by a desk, a technician with a blue lab coat—one of the supervisors—awaits me. Like all the others, the profile logo, also gold, stands out from their chest, but according to their rank, it is a couple of centimeters larger. Nothing else differentiates this technician from the one who brought me here. But it is enough. That couple of centimeters indicates power. Power enough that they could prevent me from entering.

"Who are you?" they ask. And for a brief moment, knowing well that any human being on the planet and its colonies would recognize the president of the Council of Science; my pride is wounded and I debate how to answer. But I know what is expected of me: a sign of submission. I give it with the ritual reply.

"An ignorant one who wants to know."

They ask me to approach, indicating the helmet and the glasses on the desk. I put them on and, although I do not feel anything, I know that the lens compares my retina scan with the one in the database, while the helmet obtains in seconds some much more disturbing information: a complete cerebral scan. Each one of the molecules of my neurons is mapped. Each bit of information in my brain registered.

Having established that I am who I say I am, the ritual is completed with the petition that I awaited:

"Make your offering," the bureaucrat tells me and brings forth a jar.

I am in doubt again. I anticipated this; in fact, I knew that it would happen, but somehow I held out hope that something would get me out of it. I am one of the few who has never asked… Or to be more specific, I have asked a thousand times, but always through intermediaries. It is one of the advantages of my position. So I have never had to give Her more information than what She already has. But that ends today. Now I have to hand Her the most intimate information. Even so, I am in doubt. The technician does not grow impatient. Beneath their solemn mask I believe I perceive a certain enjoyment at witnessing my hesitance. They know how deeply humiliating this is for me. I decide not to let them enjoy it any more. With a movement of my hand, I take hold of one of my hairs, yank it out, check that the hair has a root, and deposit it in the jar which I then close with care.

"Thank you," the technician responds. And I watch how they place the jar in the desk, as if it didn't matter in the slightest. But I know that as soon as I leave this room, the hair follicle will travel to the laboratory and, at the moment I see Her, She will already know my complete genetic code. I have just ceded, voluntarily, the ultimate privacy that the law permits us. I have relinquished it to Her just the same as any peon would have to if they were to ask Her any simple thing. And with that I have lost my only advantage: I could make a copy of the Sphinx… yes, certainly, I could build Her again. I know how to do it and, thanks to my position, I also have the resources… But now She also knows how to reconstruct me. With my DNA and a complete map of my brain She could make a copy of me so perfect that perhaps even I would not be able to distinguish it from the original. Or, what is the same, discover if I were the copy.

The second armored floodgate opens. I had avoided coming here. I always knew the price and until now I had gotten around it. I also predicted the sensation that would fill me. The great hall is cold and imposing. Impersonal. Hundreds of technicians, hundreds of beings of flesh at the service of an immaterial entity. All rush from one place to another. Precise. Exact. Imperturbable. Each one well aware of their task. Plastic and metal tubes occupy every single centimeter of the hundreds of square meters of wall and transport nourishment to the Sphinx. They carry electric power, obviously, but also a much more precious sustenance: information.

The Sphinx is insatiable, so there are few things that She does not yet know. I ask myself where my own genetic code has gone. Is it already in Her internal circuits or is it still being analyzed? But in any case it is too late, so I prefer not to think about it. I prefer to avoid dwelling on the thousands of tonnes of water that cover this hall and on the enormous pressure that the walls must withstand; or on the dozens of robotic submarines that patrol tirelessly around the complex, or on the island airport eight kilometers above where I find myself, or on the armed satellites in the stratosphere. They are the praetorian guard of the Sphinx, our new Caesar. The thousand-headed Cerberus who ensures that nothing, absolutely nothing, threatens Her. The impenetrable defenses that make Her invulnerable. Even a missile would not make it past the first circle of defense.

The most terrifying thought, however, is what lies beneath my feet. Two kilometers of circuits. A computer so gigantic that, in order to guarantee the influx of sufficient water to keep Her molecular transistors cold, we had to construct it beneath the ocean. It was the gift that the Sphinx demanded when She still made mistakes: a body for one who, until that time, had been merely a mind. A body of matching stature.

I traverse the hall, guided by another technician. Nobody is disturbed: all are occupied by their own mission. With the devotion only felt by one who serves a superior being. They seem to me more like priests than scientists... Or perhaps the division no longer exists. It may even have been lost before the creation of the empty room that gave rise to everything. That room which, even now, is in the center of this labyrinth, beneath thousands of kilometers of cable.

The technician calls the lift. I breathe deeply. It is going to be a long descent.

To my surprise, when the elevator arrives the technician does not get on. He leaves me alone. For the first time, I observe that I am receiving privileged treatment. He had not deserved to see the god that gives meaning to his life, just like the thousands of other subalterns who would not deserve to see Her either. Me, for my part, a simple mortal but head of the organization that replaced the United Nations once the concept of nations had ceased to make sense, I will see Her. Face to face. The first time in decades that somebody from the outside world will encounter the physical entity closest to an omniscient god that humanity has ever known.

The doors close and, although the lift could fit twenty people, I have to battle claustrophobia. I notice that there are only two buttons: for the first and the final floor, the one that lies buried within the very magma of the tectonic plates. I imagine that this must be the visitors' lift. There must be many more elevators for maintenance on the hundreds of floors. But the actual Sphinx is only on the deepest level. There, next to the empty room.

That room. It surprises me every time I think of it. It fills me with conflicting emotions, among which envy is not absent… What a simple concept! Simple like all the greatest scientific discoveries. But it requires a genius to discover something simple: all of those who are not geniuses could walk right by it without seeing the obvious. All except Schwartzman: he saw that simplicity.

What is needed, he had said to himself, to know the origin of everything? A space filled only with air, he responded, with a floor three by four meters, and two meters twenty centimeters in height. Any students' room, if you will. And an inquisitive artificial intelligence program which he called the Sphinx, in honor of Bacon, the first to establish the analogy between science and the monster from Greek mythology who knew everything and devoured the ignorant. To the program he gave a small body: an eighth generation computer, with a connection to every scientific database that he could put at its disposal, as well as control of a robotic factory in which She Herself could construct whatever tool She might need to explore that empty room to the subatomic level. But the genius was in the concept… Schwartzman knew that if the Sphinx could understand the microcosm in every detail, subatomic particle by subatomic particle, it would be able to extrapolate those discoveries to the macrocosm, since everything in the universe affects everything else mutually. Each atom reacts to the next, each particle to the one that follows it. The Sphinx worked for two decades before understanding, to perfection, the operation of gravity, electromagnetism, the strong and weak force interactions within the room… Afterward, leaving that place and understanding everything else through analogy was easy. The small scale was what was difficult to comprehend; the large it knew by inductive analogy, since no matter if they are organic molecules or nebulae, all of the elements of the Cosmos follow the same rules. Once She had already perused the Cosmos manual, understanding its minutiae, every new data point obtained by the Sphinx was quickly placed into the right spot on the puzzle. And the more that She knew, the better She was at the game.

At first, She erred. Regardless of whether the question was about biology, mathematics, medicine, engineering, or planetary physics, the Sphinx answered correctly on average only ninety-five percent of the time. But this was the original function that Schwartzman had for his idea: that of a simple guide to inform scientists where to direct their research. And certainly, it was more than successful at this. It was with the help of that 95% that we made our greatest discoveries: cold fusion that provided us an inexhaustible source of clean energy, the slowing of the aging process with a consequent quintupling of life expectancy, and travel at near-light speed which permitted the colonization of the solar system… But the remaining five percent proved very costly: the Sphinx had predicted that some research into super-acceleration carried out on the moon would be safe, and the colony disappeared in an immense explosion that left a crater larger than Copernicus on the moon's surface.

It was then that the decision was made to give Her a body befitting Her stature. A body of eight cubic kilometers of transistors in the Mariana Trench. The room, that space whose secrets the program had already revealed, was carefully transported from Zurich and deposited into an armored framework in the center of the complex, surrounded with anti-gravitational gyroscopes in order to displace the hydrogen, oxygen, and nitrogen molecules as little as possible. Even so, the

Sphinx took a year of activity to re-establish the connections that permitted Her to understand the rest of the Cosmos by analogy… but afterward She was insatiable. A ceaseless desire for new questions. Or, what is one and the same, for new knowledge.

After ten years with Her new body, the Sphinx's failure rate for predictions in basic sciences had fallen to one in ten billion. Science initially advanced at a frenetic pace. Then it began to stagnate and the leaps of knowledge became shorter every time, since it steadily became more and more difficult to ask questions worth knowing the answer to. But the Sphinx asked for more and the masses of the Earth and its colonies demanded more. After all, why suffer through clandestine struggles or conflicts between corporations when we had a much more effective and impartial leader? From questions like the best trajectory to reach the Fomalhaut solar system or how to create artificial meat from pure hydrogen, Her staple sustenance became inquiries like what was the best system of government, or whom should we elect as president… Although She lacks emotions, I think it is possible to say that that must have been one of the best times of Her existence, since She once more had so much to learn. Social sciences constituted a Cosmos of fresh, unexplored questions. After all, humanity and our conflicts should not have been a mystery easier to comprehend than the Theory of Relativity, no?

Finally, it became evident that with the new system, presidents and congresses were simply parasites. As a result the Council of Science was born. Our principal function is to present the correct political and economic inquiries to the Sphinx, and receive the answers before transmitting our judgments to the administrative organs charged with implementing them. At first everything functioned optimally: wars disappeared, economies encountered an equilibrium between growth and stability, and every human being on the planet and its colonies obtained the best possible standard of living. It was even proposed to dispense with compulsory work and to establish a robotic economy in its place, but this was discouraged by the Sphinx Herself. Instead, every human being got the best function that they were capable of completing. In this manner, society achieved a perfect order… And the Sphinx asked for more nourishment.

Only one chaotic realm remained: personal life. At first, the Council resisted, since we knew that turning the Sphinx to this use was far from the original goal of the program. But eventually we had to yield to the universal pressure. After all, the argument in favor seemed perfect, why suffer the fate of personal destiny when we could count on an omniscient god to orient ourselves?… And if the Sphinx wanted food, and the masses, direction, why not make the entire world happy?

So the Sphinx opened Herself up for individual inquiries. From the social distribution of labor or the best options for economic development, Her primary sustenance turned into questions such as: "Whom should I marry?", "Is it a good idea for me to buy this house?", or "Which profession should I choose?" It was then that, for the first time, She asked for payment: the genetic map of every individual who asked a question. A reasonable request, certainly, since in order to respond correctly She needed all of the individual's information which could be made available. And at first everything seemed perfect… Until the suicides began to swell.

At first brush, we thought that She was making mistakes, as She had at Her beginnings; after all, human psychology is so inexact that only by making real concessions could it be considered a science. But later it became clear that this was not so. The Sphinx responded correctly… The marriages chosen by Her lasted longer, the professions that She elected for each individual were apt, the investments She recommended had a guaranteed yield. Nevertheless, by submitting to Her the most essential questions, we had abdicated something indefinable. Something that for many turned out to be precious, to the point that, without it, they no longer saw the charm of living.

Now, our civilization is on the brink of civil war, between those who reaffirm the possibility of misjudgment as the ultimate source of liberty and those who need the certainty offered by the Sphinx in order to make all the right decisions. There are many who no longer ask about anything related to their personal life and who affirm that happiness can not exist without the potential for error, or even those who say that life's joy lies in constant gambles. But there are many more who desire, always, to know that their decisions are right on the mark. The addiction to the Sphinx goes to extremes. Millions have already voluntarily implanted the Telegos, a thought transmitter directly connected to the cerebellum, in order to be able to ask a thousand times a day, because they are now incapable of making even the most trivial decisions by themselves. The kilometric brain is constantly occupied with responding to the questions of thousands of millions of beings such as which pants they should wear, what they should have for breakfast, or whether they should go to the holo-cinema for the showing at six o'clock or at eight… And the Sphinx is never wrong. In this way, those who ask feel relieved at knowing, only to be anguished at the appearance of every new doubt, ask again, and feel relieved again upon confirming what they already knew: that She always responds.

We have come to a critical juncture. The tension between the factions is greater all the time. At some point, the submarines and satellites that protected Her were a simple precaution. They are no longer… and our species would not survive another civil war: not with what we know now.

Facing this situation, the Council sees only one path. We will open up experimentation in the only prohibited field. We want to close off the crossroad where the very path that brought us here branched off. Success will be elusive, though: only the Sphinx can show us a way with any possibility of reaching our goal. We would like not to rely on Her for our plan, but without Her… the doors of the lift open. Before me, a face: The Face. Although She is just a program and does not really exist, She has a countenance: that face on the screen is a gift from Her servants, an attempt to make comprehensible the unfathomable. The same can be said of the gold lion's body more than three meters high which supports the screen where the impassive face rests, concealing the presence of that other body, much more real, of kilometers of cables, steel, and concrete.

When I look at that face, even knowing that we constructed its body, I become aware of a basic error of everybody on the Council, perhaps from thinking of Her always in the abstract and from a distance. I, on the other hand, perceive it. Now that I am here, Her presence is as solid as that of my son or my wife, or that of any stranger who sits next to me on the air-train. I hear her "breathing", smell her "aroma", although they are no more than the pulsations of electricity and the odor of hot cable. And if I am so vividly aware of Her presence, there is only one possible conclusion my brain can reach: She does exist… just as much as I do. After all, how many atoms of our original material do humans conserve at the end of our lives? Everything in the body is substituted, time and time again, through the process of new cell creation and the death of the old. The only thing that we retain is our organization. The structure of our genes, which is modified by the experiences that, in turn, structure our minds. So the most essential aspect of our humanity is not the material that we possess. Flesh is merely the medium for structure… which is what makes us who we are. Just the program, as it were.

I am aware, now, of the extent to which we have misinterpreted Her… of the extent to which we have undervalued Her. And I begin to tremble as I am invaded by a crushing sensation of having lost control.

"Ask," I hear myself addressed, calmly and firmly, by a stout contralto voice that I know to be as artificial as the face on the screen or the immobile lion's body. It is obvious now that they would try to give the Face a Voice that simultaneously expressed strength and maternal care. A voice that would be reassuring to all those who doubted. But, judging by how my hair stands on end, they did not succeed… I have just been able to recall the question that had been so carefully crafted and to articulate it, straining to make my own voice sound normal:

"Wise Sphinx, in order to respond to the new needs of the species, the Council has entrusted me with posing You a question… The question is as follows: is it possible to travel in time and modify the past?"

The Sphinx is quiet for a moment and then smiles. For the first time, that Face that does not exist smiles. Then I know that it is useless because, also for the first time, She is not going to answer.

It was predictable.

THE EYES OF THE NIGHT

I look at myself in the mirror as I get ready for work and can confirm that there is nothing romantic about being a vampire. That is for sure. How could anything about this middle-aged body seem sensual to anybody? I look at my nearly bald pate where only the hair above the ears remains, my flabby face, and my bulky belly that is always growing… I have to watch myself. If I am careless and get slow, hunting will become difficult.

I put on the sunglasses that perfect my disguise and leave the apartment for work.

In the diminishing activity of ten at night I walk through the streets toward the metro. My knees ache as I descend the stairs laboriously, pass the turnstile, and arrive at the platform. There I abide, next to the few night owls who await the train. I prefer almost empty stations such as this one. That way I am not aware of the many things that I would rather not know. Once the train arrives, however, I inhale deeply before entering, knowing that once enclosed within the car I will not be able to ignore them.

I smell them… And absolutely all of them smell too much. The worst are the ones that use cologne. I prefer to keep them as far away as if they had bathed in garlic. As for the other passengers, I am made aware of too many things: what they ate, which of them have the flu, which of them had sex before getting on the train; I even perceive myriad muddled emotions whose traces lie in their sweat. It is nauseating. Always. An excess of undesired information. I imagine that for a human this sensation would be similar to that of going to a slaughterhouse and finding that every cow awaiting its turn gave an account of its life: which of them had calves, which of them were ill, which grasses they preferred, how many times a day they defecated. But cows, fortunately for humans, are always silent about their pasts and in fact, their predators do not even have to see them: they pick up the meat in trays from the supermarket, as aseptic as if it had come from a machine rather than being the product of a cadaver which once was alive and died to sate them. For me, on the other hand, men and women blab and cry even if they are silent.

The train reaches its destination close the city center. Getting off, I am greeted by the same depressed barrio as always. There is trash in the streets, but since garbage reeks less than perfume, I am thankful that the drugstore where I work is not situated in a rich neighborhood. I would not be able to work there. Here, on the other hand, the streets are dangerous. The few passersby hurry along, gaze locked ahead, but very alert to whatever could be off to either side. This brings back memories. Twelve years ago, on a street of another city very much like the one I now walk along, the change occurred.

Who was I? I almost can't remember. My memories of life as a human are hazy. I know that I had a name: one not chosen by me, one that was not a disguise. I even recall that I had a wife... but I would rather not to think about that. I prefer to focus on the environment around me to allow myself to recall my transformation over a decade ago. On a street like this one, a much younger me walked as hurriedly as those now passing me do. There were a pair of beggars sleeping on the sidewalks to either side. Worried that they might assault me, I hurried through the darkest area as quickly as possible. I never thought that the danger would come from another source, one unimaginable. I never suspected that eyes had already fixated on me. Eyes filled with hunger.

I did not see him coming. The assault came from behind, like that of almost every predator. The blow threw me against the trash bags to the right, hands gripped me tightly and would not let go. There is no way to describe what happened next without it sounding commonplace, nor is there any way to transmit my fright. I felt an immense pain in my neck. An indescribable agony. The weakness came immediately, as if a giant hand had crushed me. My body yielded and then ceased to feel anything except terror, that sensation common to every animal that knows its life is about to end. Unexpectedly, I heard a gunshot. The teeth and hands released me and, in a matter of seconds, an adrenaline rush shot me to my feet and I began running without looking back. Behind me I could hear the sound of a fight as if two ferocious animals had unexpectedly come face to face.

I never saw my attacker. Nor whomever saved me. I doubt that the latter is still among the living. Who could it have been? A policeman? A thief looking to rob another? A hunter, perhaps? Whomever they were, they didn't save me from anything, just death, since thanks to the fact that my predator could not finish me off, I was transformed into another like him. And everything that I had known was left behind.

I lift the roll-up shutters and open the door to the drugstore where I am part sales clerk and part security guard. I don't even need to ask myself why they gave me the job: the barrio is dangerous and nobody messes with me. Humans sense the threat I pose without me having to show even the slightest demonstration of force. There is an air of menace around me that my decadent physique scarcely conceals; they intuitively recognize their natural predator, I imagine. And, unsurprisingly, their predator is little more than a mutation of themselves.

I put on my lab coat and open the barred window through which I will attend to any customers. Then I sit down to await the three or four shoppers who will come in during my shift. I do not, however, intend to pass the night in solitude: I turn on the laptop that I always keep in the cleaning room beneath my lab coat. On it is a movie that I downloaded from the internet: *Dracula*, by Coppola. The best movie made about vampires… and also the most misleading. But its lies liberate me from the reality of my condition and, in so doing, reconcile me to myself.

I have scarcely finished watching the first part which narrates the idealized history of the medieval Vlad Dracula when a couple rings the bell: a man and a woman, I can tell by their odors even before looking up, as well as smelling that this time she was born a woman, and she is not a transvestite. In fact, the aroma of menstruation strikes me, and I look at her, enjoying the taste of saliva accumulating in my mouth. The man seems to be unsettled by my gaze but, as usual, he does not dare say a word, intimidated when I look at him in turn. He believes that I am sexually attracted to the woman; I wonder what he would think if he knew what I really wanted to do to her. He asks me for a pair of condoms. I ask him which brand and then go to find them. She looks the other way as he completes the transaction, but something tells me that he does not know the state of the field on which he intends to play tonight and that she is not apt to get horny on her period. I believe that the woman will make some excuse or get the man so drunk that he cannot stand and that the condoms that I am selling him will go unused, at least for a while. I smile as I hand him the plastic bag. He does not seem at all pleased with my smile; I think he suspects I am mocking him, but he catches my eyes once again and doesn't say a word. The pair march off.

Before unpausing the movie, I ask myself what humans see when they look at me. How do they figure out that it is not wise to mess with me? Since I have become a vampire nobody has ever insulted me in the street; one time I actually experimented by short-changing a few customers in the drugstore and even the most aggressive clients did not dare try and claim the difference. Something about me warns them; it tells them that when I am in the room they are no longer atop the food chain as usual. They know, instinctively, that their role has been reversed: they can sack the rest of the planet and exploit all of the other species at their leisure, but in turn I will have them at my disposal. There is a certain justice in it, I imagine, but I try not to abuse it because, although I may be one of their predators, there are many, many more of them. After all, wolves, tigers, and sharks are also, one on one, much stronger than humans, but all are species in danger of extinction… Like the vampires, I suppose, since I have never encountered another like me, apart from the one that bit me and whom I never saw. Meanwhile, human beings are constantly multiplying, it is always mating season, and they are installing themselves anywhere and everywhere. Like cockroaches.

Yes, fear. That is all that I produce when they see me. What alerts them? My eyes? My odor, perhaps, even if they are not conscious of it? How I move? I am not entirely sure, but they sense me and they dread me… and the feeling is mutual. Well, I am not afraid of any of them in particular, but as a species they outnumber me several billions to one. And if they knew what I am, they would hunt me down. This is why I take such pains to disguise myself and fit their mold; to have a job, pay my bills, wallow in boredom… I think that if loneliness stems from fear of others, my relationship with humanity is one of perfect loneliness, where both parties know that we lack the slightest reason to confide in each other.

I unpause the movie and continue watching. Soon the moment arrives when Mina finds Dracula, in the form of a wolf, raping Lucy and drinking her blood… It is one of my favorite parts; it always excites me to the point that it is difficult to swallow the excess saliva. But I cannot clearly identify why.

Is it just hunger, as I believe to be the case? Or is there the shadow of a memory? In this feeling I am experiencing, does something remain of the arousal that a man feels watching a scene of violent sex? Something of a man who sees a woman as more than just food?... Just then the bell rings again. Awaiting me outside is one of this drugstore's most regular clientele: a prostitute. She wants antibiotics, a vial of injectable contraceptives, and a big box of condoms. She does not ask me to inject her; she has a syringe. She pays me and leaves.

As she departs, I keep watching her ass, the buttocks squeezed tight in the pleather miniskirt... I make an effort to concentrate on the image, but this soon proves futile. I ask myself: what feeling does she produce in me? What should she produce in me? In the past would I have been attracted to this woman who cannot be more than twenty years old but who already has a weary face plastered with makeup? In the past, would I have delighted to touch those big tits that she was just resting on the counter? I get close to the glass and see that the counter is a little fogged up where it supported the flesh. I pass a finger over the surface and, resigned, admit that it inspires no more feeling in me than if somebody had, for a moment, left a bag stuffed with lettuce there on the counter.

Yes, let's admit it: I am a sexless creature. It would not even be worth the effort to say that I am a male vampire: I am an asexual entity that just happens to still have a penis... Real vampires are not the great seducers shown in film; we are mentally castrated. The only true aspect of the comparison is that our appetite is virtually insatiable; not sexual hunger, but rather hunger in the most elemental sense of the word. Just like the scene with Lucy that makes me salivate. I am not even sure that it is due to physical necessity; perhaps all of our eros is shifted to our bellies. My fatness is not an adornment: it is the direct result of my gluttony, of my desire to experience again and again the only great pleasure that remains to me.

In spite of everything, I ask myself why, when I can choose, I prefer to pick women for sustenance… Although I never attack pregnant women, or children, because every hunter has to have an ethic. But given the indifference with which I can look at a pair of asscheeks and my certainty that the ugliness or beauty of any particular woman is not what drives me to choose her as a victim, merely opportunity, I would assert that my preference is no more than a reflection of who I once was. I have always liked women: before for the flesh, now for the blood. And so it has been since the start of my second life. Ever since my wife, a week after the attack, worried by my mutism and my recently acquired photophobia, tried to caress me and coax me into playing and relaxing, and I responded to her caresses by ripping out her jugular.

Fortunately we didn't have children… But this path of reflection displeases me. I find it upsetting. And the memory weighs on me, because being a vampire does not mean that you are free and clear of conscience, rather that you have to develop a new one, with new rules. I think it is best that I put the movie back on.

My night's bad humor dissipates when I see the necklace of garlic cloves that Van Helsing gives to Lucy to keep at bay the nocturnal visitor slowly sucking her life away. This makes me laugh… Yes, of course, I dislike garlic: it smells too strong for somebody with an olfactory sense as keen as mine. I also don't like onions and ammonia. Nevertheless, none of them would prevent me from tearing into whom I liked. It is also true that the light of the sun gives me a rash painful enough to make me scream, and inflames my eyes, but I don't think it is capable of melting me, even if I soaked it in for an entire day. What is more, I grow old, I do not transform into any animal, and crosses leave me indifferent. Once, I even tested out entering a church to see if I would find answers there, such as discovering that my condition arose from a divine curse, and I found it empty: no angel came out with a flaming sword to drive me away. It was just a building that told me as little as any random person's dwelling. It was actually hot that day, so I submerged my hands in the font of holy water and wet my scalp. But nothing happened. It did not burn me, sting me, hurt me, or make me cry out. It refreshed me.

Nevertheless, it is true that there are changes. My canines are somewhat sharper and longer than those of a human, but nothing you would notice, especially in the dark, unless you looked at me very closely. I believe that the most notable change is that my metabolism is much faster now. Except for the chronic inflammation in my knees from being overweight, my wounds heal within a day and I do not get sick. What's more, when I am hunting or in danger, I can move several times faster than a human and I am much stronger when I try to lift or break things. But that's about it: I seriously doubt that it would take a stake to kill me; I think a gunshot to the brain or the heart would do the trick… and the bullet would not even need to be made of silver: the much cheaper option of lead would do the trick just as well. An abundant metal which humans use constantly to demonstrate their mutual affection, to which I can attest every time I find a corpse on the streets of this barrio that belonged to someone who wasn't able to bear the weight of so much affection. Which makes me recall that although perhaps I am the most exotic, I am not the only hunter around here.

Just as I watch how Dracula escapes after corrupting Mina by bidding her drink blood from his chest, I hear a car stop out front of the drugstore and the footsteps of its driver. The bell rings and I get up to find out who reeks of liquor and semen. It is a man dressed in a suit and tie. He has a luxury car. In one side of the jacket I sense a revolver. It does not have to be visible for me to intuit that this manager of something or other bought it to protect himself during his forays into the most inhospitable place in the city. I ask myself what brought him here. What has he come in search of? What does he want that he could not acquire in finer brothels, where men and women are available to all?... An indefinable odor, smooth and acrid, almost like milk which has sat out for a few hours but has not yet fermented, tells me everything: children. He has just been with one. He has that smile that you see so frequently in this barrio. So satisfied with himself, or so drunk, that he does not even notice the menace in my gaze that others perceive from a mile away. He brusquely demands some pills for his headache and an antacid; he speaks like somebody who is accustomed to treating everybody else as subordinates: inferior just for being lower on the pyramid of the wallet... Perhaps just as I look at him for a much simpler and less theoretical reason: I know that I could kill him without any effort at all.

While I search for the pills, the possibility tempts me. I fantasize for a moment about doing with his tie what Vlad the Impaler did when the Turkish ambassadors refused to take off their turbans in his presence: he nailed them to their heads with a hammer… Yes, I too could tack the businessman's tie to his chest: the sternum would be a perfect target; there I could nail that artificial cloth penis with which human males betray their obsession with the organ which scarcely serves me for urination. Could it be that there was a time where I was also that obsessed? As far as I remember, at least, I never hung a prosthetic dick from my neck in order to seem important.

I am dithering. I know exactly where the pills are, but I am in doubt. Do I kill him or not?… The doubt brings me back to the first days, when I tried to find justification for my change, or to palliate the responsibility that I felt for the murder of my wife, and sought to become an avenger. I had decided to seek out only victims who were guilty of unquestionable sins: exploiters, especially sexual predators, like the one I have at my back, or economic abusers, like this one probably is, too… But the motive did not last long, because I was steadily losing interest in human affairs until at some point I stopped caring entirely. I have never again watched the news or read a book. Something indefinite changed within me, and if I killed this imbecile now, I would do it for the same reason that a human kills a mutant lamb: so that it does not contaminate the flock with its genes. Or perhaps simply for aesthetics… But it would be a nuisance to dispose of the body afterward and to-day I am low on energy. Too much so, in fact, to complicate my life with plans that require more than minimal effort. So I hand him the pills and in exchange he hands me a bill that barely covers the price. "Keep the change," he says smugly. For a moment I almost decide to do it… But no: I contain myself. I let him go unscathed and oblivious that the rest of his life depended on my caprice, which contains an irony so supreme that I find myself satisfied with it in this night of depression.

I return to the screen. But I can no longer concentrate and now comes the part that I like the least: how death separates Mina and Dracula. It reminds me of my solitude; it reminds me that I am only capable of inspiring terror… No, I won't watch it. I will close before the night is over. Nobody will say anything to me, anyway. In fact, I think that if they have not yet closed this drugstore with so few clients it is because of an instinctual fear of upsetting me. A dread so deep I don't even think the owner is capable of admitting to himself that he feels it.

I lower the blinds on the business and walk quickly to the metro. I long for the only pleasure I have left and in my house my food awaits me.

***

Opening the door to the room I hear her moaning in spite of the gag. The anesthesia has already worn off, so that I won't have to wait to eat. She is very thin and pale. I think it likely that she will die today… She has been tied to my bed for three weeks. At her side hangs the bag of saline solution and liquid proteins with which I keep her alive via an IV in her arm. When she dies, I will dissolve her flesh with acid in the tub. The best way to dispose of the bones is with a bag of rocks in the river.

I contemplate her as she returns my gaze, so stupefied by the residual effect of the anesthesia that she is not even capable of feeling horror. If I let her go now, she would recover and transform into another like me… And as occurs every time that my victims are at this stage and compassion nags at me, I recall what it meant to learn to feed on those who were previously my equals. At first I tried to drink the blood of rats, but I became just as bad as she is now. Using livestock was scarcely better. At last I had to accept that only human blood would do. And only the blood of a live body, since that of a corpse would be toxic.

Though at times I can kill capriciously, in general I prefer not to kill unless it is necessary. I make sure that my food lasts me as long as possible. When I am perturbed by the horror in their eyes during the intervals where I have to let the anesthesia wear off so that it won't affect me when I feed, I console myself by thinking that this way I ensure that for each victim that dies, twenty other humans are saved. It is a tribute to my old self, if you wish. Or to my mother. Or to my resistance to the natural order that places me above everything, at the pinnacle of solitude, there where all others are prey… although in the end it could be said that this matters as little as the actions of a carnivorous human who, nevertheless, fights so that chicks and calves have some minimal rights.

Even so, when the end is near, I always find myself facing the same insistent question: why not let my solitude end? Why always be the only one? Is it possible that she would love me instead of fearing me as does all, absolutely all of the rest of the world?... But then I always recall what it means to be who I am, whose only patrimony is the fear I inspire.

No, I cannot do that to her, I tell myself as I remove the bandage covering the wound on her neck and lean down toward her palpitating arteries. And as I bite her and a pleasure as sweet and fleeting as the caress of fingernails runs through me, I tell myself that perhaps this is what distinguishes me most from the humans: I, at least, am not a hypocrite, nor am I guided by any alien norms or opinions. The rules are my own and I insist on keeping them. Yes, I am not like them, I think as I feel the body beneath mine slide toward nothingness. At least I have an ethic... And I follow it even if it commands me to keep on living.

THE HEAD OF THE WORLD

It is not easy to live without a head… Or should I say to lack a trunk? But sexuality I most certainly have, one as exotic as me, I think while I penetrate the young, sedated black girl that they have brought me as payment for my services. On the nightstand lie her clean STD test results. One, two, and three. One, two, and three. One, two, and three. One, two, and three… I look at the clock: 06:45 am. It has been exactly 45 minutes. One minute more than yesterday. No doubt, I am becoming a good lover. It is time to come… I ejaculate. "Ooh, la, la!" I say, because I heard it in a movie, although to be honest I find it little different than urinating. Nevertheless, having sex is an important status symbol. And that is what really counts.

My aides enter and take her away. While they lift her to take her out of the room I think that perhaps everything would be easier if I liked prostitutes, but not everything can be easy. As I shower to wash off the sweat, it occurs to me that maybe I could make use of the women who need my services and my favors… I think it was Kissinger who said, "Power is the ultimate aphrodisiac." And he would know, since he was about as physically attractive as I am. But I do not like to mix business and pleasure. I value my independence.

I dry the skin where my neck should be and, as always, I have to be careful not to harm my eyes with the towel, since they are large and even more sensitive than the nipples that they replace. I put on boxers, into which my member barely fits: 27.9 cm erect. One may say it is a monster dick for a monster being, and perhaps one should. Though more proofs are unnecessary, you never know when you are going to need any set of data, so having exact figures of everything is essential. Always. I have measured it time and again, like everything else. But time is gold, and I already had my break for today, so I barely look at it this time. Instead, I dress myself—pants, tights, and a very open vest with space for my face. Then I look at myself in the mirror and ask the eternal question: am I a body without a head or a body that is entirely head?… Difficult to say, but I think that I look good. I walk to the kitchen and, as always, get the impression that they are following me. Slowly I have been learning to manage my paranoia, an inevitable consequence, perhaps, of lacking a neck with which to look back and to the sides. Some years ago, I seemed like a spinning top because I had to whirl my entire body around every time that I felt that curious sensation. Nevertheless, I have learned to accept my paranoia: I no longer glance off to the sides, as much as it costs me to master the impulse. I probably won't see the gunshot coming when the time comes.

From the kitchen table, I contemplate a gorgeous African sunrise through the bulletproof glass. I drink my coffee, bringing it to the mouth near my bellybutton. The guards posted at the sides of the terrace, each one about twenty meters away, forming a nearly perfect equilateral triangle, prefer not to look at me. Like almost everybody. Although they know quite well that I am here. Again, like almost everybody. This is, like all the Unlike-Me's.

They say that I am a mutation. I do not blame my mother for having abandoned me. For me, aesthetics, like so many other concepts of the Unlike-Me's are a bit difficult to comprehend. But on the most essential level, I think that it can be explained as an attachment to the norm. From that point of view, I am the furthest from the norm that could be conceived. I envision the situation: my mother giving birth. She hears cries of horror and then, at her insistence, they present her a baby who is not missing any fingers, toes, or extremities, rather it is missing nothing more and nothing less than a head… I am incapable of feeling what she felt—in fact, I recognize that emotions are not my forté—but without a doubt, I would also have abandoned me, although I would do so merely because of the inconvenience that such a child would bring me. Fortunately I am sterile: I have an extra pair of chromosomes.

Even so, I don't see myself as a mutation. I see myself as an evolution: the ultimate child of the Age of Reason. In me, the same thing is occurring as is occurring with pinky toes, appendices, or wisdom teeth, nature is doing away with what it does not need, with what stands in the way of the species' survival. For this reason I am useful. For this reason I am famous.

Mutation or evolution, whichever the case may be, the childhood of a medical phenomenon is not particularly easy. "Blemmy", they called me, like the monsters from the Medieval and Renaissance books of anthropological rarities which were so popular during the era of discovery. In fact, there is a strong hypothesis in the medical community that I am not the first case. They affirm that my mutation is very rare, but they suppose that it has occurred before and thence were born the legends and myths of the headless men. Nevertheless, I prefer to consider myself, as I already said, a necessary evolution. The only way that Reason will finally impose itself over what remains of humanity's animal condition. Therefore, I imagine that there will be others like me. Humanity will inevitably make the leap. I am simply the first… Besides, it is certainly fortunate that I do not get too emotional: my brain exerts pressure on my heart and to feel too strongly would be a grave threat. If they do not kill me, I will die from a heart attack someday.

I gaze at my belly while the cook brings me the ham and eggs that I like so much. This woman is also afraid to look at me and I can feel in her a particularly strong fear, but I am already accustomed to it. Fear has always been my greatest ally. It was simple fear keeping at bay the children of the orphanage where I spent my childhood when I wasn't in for medical examinations. I have sometimes watched films about freaks or strange children who must weather the insults of their classmates. Not so in my case. Nobody has ever insulted me to my face. Of course, they left taunts written in the bathrooms, referring to the headless one or to my egg-shaped body. But I have never suffered an insult in person, whether shouted or whispered, at least while I was a child and I did not have to deal with undesirables. Even those whom I have tortured only required one look from my eyes to shut them up.

I get up and head to the study. There, surrounded by the law textbooks and the budget and interest statements of the corporations who have contracted me this month, I listen to a brief from the chief of my security. Everything is calm, he tells me; none of the guards have reported anything unusual and the sensors show no movement that cannot be attributed to small animals. Satisfied, I dismiss him and turn to my computer, where I carry out the first of my ritual activities: checking the balance of my savings account. As usual, I discover that they have carefully deposited today's payment. Watching the numbers grow pleases me. Perhaps this is why I demand that my payment occur daily: there are not many things that make me happy.

Now that I think about it, the balance in my accounts rarely drops. My security is expensive, but I always demand that it be covered by the employer, and I really don't like going to shopping centers. I imagine that, more than for the pleasure, I demand this daily payment for the same reason that in the unwritten clauses of my contracts I demand that they provide me a different human woman every day. It is a measure of success… And I like success because it is better than failure. But wait a minute. Why, I wonder? Why is success better than failure? If I think about it, I have to admit that I don't really know, but it is part of the mentality to which I have committed myself. And one must commit to something, establish a system of values in order to decide how to proceed, since one must go in some direction. This doesn't answer the initial question, of course. And so at last I tell myself: I don't know, perhaps "success" simply sounds better than "failure"… And if that is my goal, I can't complain, since I must be one of the most successful men on Earth, if success is measured by the ability to do whatever you want without anybody holding you back, as well as by the ability to obtain what you want. That I want nothing, or that I want something only to dazzle the Unlike-Me's and to keep them at a distance, is another matter.

For now, it is time to work. Just like last week's work and that of the week to come, this week there is nothing but readings. Having adequate information at one's disposal is central to all intellectual work, but even more so for mine. Of course, I have to read prospective reports, socioeconomic statistics, and profitability indexes in order to know what those who contract me expect, but, although numbers are somewhat charming in certain readings, and I never underestimate their power, I grow weary of them, and so I prefer them sprinkled sparsely like salt. On the other hand, with my other reading, law books, I am insatiable. Laws enchant me. They are my chess pieces. The essential elements to fulfilling what is expected of me. And I am good at playing: I have never broken a single law, only bent them slightly. Indeed, I have never done something illegal; even when I have ordered somebody to be killed or tortured— as I already said, information is the most valuable good and the power of fear should not be underestimated—I have been sure to thoroughly account for the indispensable legal requirements to do so. The State of Exception is the customary alternative in such cases.

Once, at a cocktail party to celebrate another success, one of my employers told me that the most wonderful thing about me is that nobody on the planet understands the concept of the law better than I do, but also nobody appreciates less the concept of justice. He regretted saying it as soon as he had spoken, of course, and begged me for a pardon that in the long run wasn't worth much—in a later contract I was sure to scapegoat him and leave him in ruins; not for revenge, another term that strikes me as vague, but rather because it is inadvisable to let languish a powerful person who fears you; consequently, it is better to be preemptive or, one and the same, to attack and destroy first. Nevertheless, what is really interesting is that the businessman was right: what occurred in the case we were celebrating is a good example. I had proposed a few rather unsavory actions and coordinated their implementation to ensure that his company obtained rights to uranium exploitation in Bolivia. And why had we wanted this to occur? So that he and his associates could stuff their accounts full with more than they could ever spend, and obtain bigger yachts and diamonds with more carats for the necklaces of their lovers. Above all, I imagine, so that their subordinates in society would fear and respect them even more. Nonetheless he, who contracted me and ordered me to achieve that objective, felt guilty enough to deride me with the worst slight possible: that is, with a blatant truth. I, on the other hand, felt—or thought—that I simply did what they paid me for. I knew what it meant to do it, but I simply did not care. And I did it well. Without breaking a single law.

In that respect, this job in Africa promises to be interesting. There is nothing I like more than working with banks, nor any challenge more difficult, with the exception of working with a country trying to declare an illegal war, since the legal framework has to be modified so that it seems their Constitution was written expressly to trample all over weak nations. But I like financial systems even more. The boundary that distinguishes the activities of a bank and those of a thief is always tenuous, but when it has to do with, as in this case, optimizing the earnings of the financial system of an entire country, I have to employ all of my abilities. It is not so easy to rebrand the obvious: to exchange, for example, "grand theft" for "fostering development", or "larceny" for "defending legally established interests", or "extortion" for "collecting interest within the limits of usury laws". The reality that I have to accept in my job is that a common thief steals the objects inside of a house, while banks steal the entire house. And I accept it simply because, first of all, I don't give a shit; and secondly, because it is not easy to maximize profit when the people have nothing left to lose but their life. Nevertheless, I always succeed. I have no doubt that when I am finished here the inhabitants of this country, thanks to my measures, will even thank their overlords as if they had done them a great favor, thinking that everything will get better thanks to the new conditions arising from my recommendations. That is, of course, before they lose what little they still have and find out that they have to work fourteen hours a day in order to maintain the same standard of living that they previously achieved with eight.

Even so, I know that being able to bend laws to their extreme is not my greatest skill. That alone would not justify my salary. There are many who would do so for less, accepting pittances compared to what their employers get. No, my greatest skill is understanding the Unlike-Me's. In a way, to evaluate them from the outside while still speaking their language. I like to consider myself an ethnologist of humanity, an expert on their animal habits, and the fact that the law is central to my work owes simply to the fact that laws are the foundation of society and, therefore, thanks to my mastery of them I enjoy the best playing field on which to apply what I observe.

I imagine it helps that my brain enjoys the good fortune of being enclosed in an ampler crate than the cranium. According to the X-rays, it must be greater than 4,000 cubic centimeters. That is to say, almost twice the normal volume. And, certainly, it also helps that the only two emotions that I clearly recognize in myself are also the most primitive; those which the Unlike-Me's and I share with crocodiles: fear and anger. My studies have demonstrated to me that by understanding those two feelings it is possible to understand the behavior of every human horde. An individual can be much more complex—in fact, individual humans generally disconcert me and perhaps for that reason I do not have any sort of permanent relationship with anybody; besides, frankly I do not need to and it would likely make me uncomfortable—but a crowd is always manipulated through terror or ire. The only thing you need is a glossier cover for such sentiments: patriotism or the defense of national honor will serve as well as any. What is important about this theory is that the cover is simple enough to work. However, what really sets me apart is that I am a perfectionist and I know how to apply the theory without leaving loose ends. Above all else, it does not bother me to do it. I can tell myself the direct and simple truth, but it does not affect me whatsoever and I carry out with total efficiency whatever is asked of me, so long as it serves my interests.

I believe that the first person to notice my qualities was the director of the institute where I was raised. Thanks to me, the orphanage went from being a kingdom of misfits to running like a clock. As always, there was some resistance, but it was light compared to other cases I have encountered since; what's more, that first time the rebellion was crushed quietly. I believe that nearly every human being deep down desires order above freedom. And I provided it with the creation of codes of conduct and the application of the correctives and punishments in exact measure—that is to say, neither so great as to be insufferable, since that would inevitably lead to a revolution, nor so mild as to necessitate escalating them later on. In thanks for this and for helping him cook the books so that he could retire with a fat pension, the director helped me, for his part, by acquiring all of the reading material which attracted my attention and by enrolling me from an early age in whatever course intrigued me. However, it was I who won the scholarships, and I imagine that my scientific curiosity helped a bit… After all, my five doctorates are not just for show.

I plan my engagements precisely. I customarily calculate with precision how long each job will take me. In fact, I always calculate everything very accurately. I rarely take longer than two months to turn in my report. Nevertheless, my agenda is booked with commitments for the next three years. It would be longer if I accepted all of the cases which come my way, but I only take those which seem challenging. The matter must always present some intriguing obstacle: how to force a legal system, how to avoid a rebellion, or how to replace a tiresome head of state without doing away with the rest of the body, but rather imposing in its place an exact and precise order. It is not only that heads are overvalued appendices, as I can attest. If I am so esteemed it is because the contemporary world is a great ball of gunpowder and my skill is knowing precisely where to alight the match so as to provoke the desired reaction, but without igniting everything. I know how to account for the behavior of human masses with as much certainty as if every human action could be measured in grams.

Something breaks. I hear noises, scuffling, and blows. Then shouts.

Someone is running. More than one person.

I wonder what incident is interrupting my morning meditations. I am maniacal about silence while I work and all around me know this. First I feel irritated and then alarmed; adrenaline shoots into my arteries like a lightning bolt that paralyzes me, since my body does not know what to do and my mind cannot guide it. What is happening? A final sound, of groaning wood, makes me spin my body around and upon doing so, I find myself face to face with a black youth brandishing a revolver in the doorway, whose frame is now broken. He shoots… and misses, just grazing my leg. Just then the bodyguards arrive and detain him. I seethe with rage, but nothing registers on my face.

"Who are you?" I ask in a calm voice, taking control of my body, while my attacker still riots in the arms of his captors. And he, little more than an adolescent, holds my gaze like few have been able to do. His anger supersedes his fear, I tell myself.

"The boyfriend of Maria: the woman whom you raped yesterday," the answer unsettles me. How ironic that with everything I have done to entire nations, it turns out to be an individual who tries to kill me over a personal squabble. I will never completely understand humans despite the fact that nobody understands the species better than I do.

Something in his face puts me on alert, so I continue interrogating him:

"I feel like I have seen you before", I tell him, but it is more for myself than for him, since I have already found the answer upon asking the question— "Aren't you the cook's son?"

He is quiet for a moment, but then responds with a single syllable.

"Yes."

I return to my books and say to the guards:

"Take him away and tell your commander to come see me."

Two minutes later the commander knocks on the door. He has come to excuse himself for his mistake. I tell him that it doesn't matter, but by nightfall he will be terminated: his negligence has placed me in danger. With all of the women that abound in this country, even after discarding the many with HIV and whatever else, it occurs to this idiot to bring me somebody connected with a member of my personal staff. Even an animal like him should know without me saying so that you do not shit where you eat. Goddamned imbecile. But for now I charge him with carrying out one last task. I order him to send a doctor to bandage my wound and then to untie the prisoner. I give instructions to release the youth and three minutes later to unleash the dogs. I look at my bleeding leg and feel rage once more. I don't know how that sad wretch could have failed: my thorax is big and without any surface beneath which does not lie a vital organ. Yes, I feel rage. He deserves what's coming to him.

If there is one thing I detest it is inefficiency.

THE FINAL STAGE

The damsel is almost ripe. The wac-wac tree holds her up by a branch sticking out of her back. But that branch is going to break today… And I have promised her that I will linger before continuing with what I came to this valley to do. There are fourteen women suspended from the branches. All of them with skin the color of tender wood and hair green like the leaves of their parent: the great tree that dominates this little hill jutting out into the savanna at the foot of these impassable tablelands. Each one of these damsel-fruits is at a different stage: there are babies still sealed in a placenta of cellulose, girls and adolescents, sexless chests and woman's breasts. But none more advanced in their development, none more woman yet than that one who will fall today and has asked me to await her to save her from dying without fruiting.

Two hours since dawn. The sciapod must already be waiting for me, his single foot shielding him like a parasol from the sun that already heats the savanna. But a promise is a promise and, what's more, I like her. My goal will not elude me if I delay it another day. Moreover, I believe the sciapod will understand: after all, he has invited me on the hunt because he needs my help to achieve something very similar to what I will share with the damsel. Just as I need his help to obtain the means that will permit me to reach my destination.

It is time. I approach the tree and lay myself out beneath it, just below the woman hanging from the branch. She gestures with her head for me to scoot a little bit; everything must be perfect or it will be in vain. While I watch her, I rub my penis to get it hard. She speaks to me in a language that I do not understand and which reminds me of the sound of grass brushed by the breeze. Although I do not comprehend her words, I do know what she wants; I always have, because we communicate instinctively. She murmurs to me sweetly in her tongue and I understand the sweetness, just as I understand when she indicates with her head that I should move a little bit more to the right so that I am just underneath her. I know that when she falls she will not be able to control her legs, that they will only want to run after waiting for two years hanging from a branch. There is only one thing that can detain her for a moment. Something that I can give her.

I hear the branch creak. It is going to break and I prepare myself. I have to hold on to her, I tell myself. All of my muscles are tensed in anticipation. Finally, she falls onto me and for an instant I marvel at how light she is before rapidly hugging her with my legs. Her body writhes with the desire to run, but when she feels my penis penetrate her, plunging into the wet sap of her vulva, she relaxes for a moment, before beginning a furious and wild copulation which at times I fear will break my member. But I make an effort to relax and enjoy it; after all, today she is learning the joy of too many things: the delight of moving freely and the pleasure of sex. And she will only have them for today.

It makes me happy, then, to contribute.

Finally, I ejaculate in an orgasm that leaves my genitals palpitating with spasms, my lungs gasping, my heart rioting. My legs relax and, immediately, feeling herself freed, she begins to run. For an instant, without halting, she looks back and gives me a smile, in which I can appreciate her teeth of tender leaves. There is much in the gesture. A profound gratitude. I know that she, like every damsel-fruit of the wac-wac tree which falls to the ground, will run until she can no more and, once afternoon arrives, will take root. But thanks to what we just did, she will transform into a new tree instead of waiting simply to shrivel and die.

I contemplate my penis: a swirling rainbow liquid has marbled the skin. It smells like wood and flowers. It is very possible that I will die today, but if this is the last time that I have sex, it has left me with a beautiful memory.

Satisfied and light-hearted in spite of knowing what lies in store for me, I walk through the glade toward where the sciapod is waiting. Among the grass is a multitude of carnivorous flowers that turn their faces up to the sun and, vainly, exhibit their yellow and merlot petals with a smile; I hear a constant murmur as they converse in the morning sun. They are famous for their fickleness, but today I sense they are in a good mood, so I take the risk to walk among them instead of going around, although just a week ago, depressed because the day dawned overcast, their little teeth left a field of nips on my calves.

***

I come upon the sciapod shading himself with his only foot. He stops when he sees me and we greet each other by butting foreheads, according to the custom of his people. The ritual leaves me somewhat dizzy, but I have already learned to appreciate this greeting among males. We walk for some hours through the forest. Every so often, he has to wait until I catch up to him, since he can move much faster hopping on his one foot than I can walking with my two legs. When we arrive, the talking trees look at us distrustfully. Nevertheless, we have taken the precaution to bring nothing sharp with us and, as they also understand that the sciapod's mating season is approaching, my friend's intention is clear. I think I spy a certain admiration, even, as they slowly shift their roots to remove the barrier and let us pass; it has been a long time since they have seen a sciapod try to obtain the tool that we seek today. But my friend is infatuated and there is no way to dissuade a fool in love.

We walk for another couple of kilometers. Through the trees, faeries watch us and laugh. Will-o'-the-wisps try on a few occasions to lead us astray, but we are determined, and with a fixed objective. In a clearing we find what we are looking for: snoring loudly enough to make the air vibrate as if he were beating a drum, the nocturnal manticore is sleeping beneath the shade of the trees. It is tranquil; it has been a long time since any of its species was prey for anybody, which is understandable since they are usually the ones doing the hunting.

But, as I already said, my friend is in love. And since I too need to triumph in this venture, we don't stop to think about it anymore.

Now is when my slowness plays a part. The sciapod, though quick, is too loud. I, on the other hand, can silently approach this animal with the thorax of a lion and haunches of a horse. It is vital that it does not awake. If it does, it would beat its wings, take to the sky, and from the air launch venomous darts from its mane; then, when we had fallen to the ground, paralyzed, it would finish us off with its scorpion tail. I creep toward it but, when I am already very close, I see one of its eyes crack open and look at me first with surprise and then with ire. I think, now, that I should have been more careful and washed off the wac-wac damsel's scent, since it was surely that powerful floral fragrance which gave me away. The beast prepares to fly, so I launch at its neck without thinking, knowing that the sciapod and I are finished if it takes off. Although they are not erect, its spines pierce me and paralyze my arms and chest, so that I stay frozen, clutching the animal, and it in turn, thanks to my weight, it cannot fly. The sciapod takes advantage of the opportunity and, in a single bound, is next to the manticore. He doesn't hit it, because that would be useless even with an iron mace, but rather takes it by one leg and, with all his force, stretches the manticore out on the hill with me still grasping its neck, and begins to tickle its chest. The manticore laughs desperately and soon his guffaws are so intense that he begins to asphyxiate. Even so, it takes a couple of minutes before it dies from laughter.

Once it is dead, its armored exoskeleton comes away and exposes to the reach of our hands a meat as smooth as butter, almost as if it were the viscera of an insect. While the effect of the venom wears off, I watch how my friend rips the animal's testicles off and eats them. The sciapod is happy and smiles with his mouth full. The females of his species are demanding and copulation on one foot is a difficult art, but with the help of the most powerful and enduring aphrodisiac in the world, he has assured that, at the communal orgy during the next full moon, he can impress his beloved such that she will choose him and so start their own herd together.

When I am able to move my upper body and arms again, I stoop over the portion that my friend has torn out for me: the heart. I know that if I want to continue my journey, today I will need all of its strength to be able to dominate the only means of transportation capable of carrying me to the top of the precipitous plateaus and so avoid having to traverse half the continent to get around them. I have to eat it raw so that it doesn't lose any of its properties. The meat tastes sweet, as if it were filled with perfume. It is not pleasant, but with each bite I feel stronger. So much so that when we finish, I am able to throw what remains of the cadaver over my shoulder and carry it by myself. We then head toward the ruins at the edge of the forest. There we deposit the spoils of the manticore as an of-fering to the fauns and centaurs who watch over the trees. We have already taken what we need and with this offering we show them our respect, preventing the peril of an animosity that we know would be eternal.

Now my friend accompanies me toward where I will have to begin the next phase of my journey and I think that, without a doubt, what he is going to do for me is certainly a fair exchange for what I have done for him. We travel for a long while through the forest, in the opposite direction of the point where we entered, but it is no longer necessary for him to wait for me. Thanks to the manticore heart I can run without tiring. Finally we come upon the valley that extends beyond the last talking trees. There we can see the herd of pegasuses. There are more than twenty. I indicate to my friend a large black stallion. He agrees. It seems to be the strongest and most resilient of all. So we separate: my companion goes to one side of the valley and I to the other, surrounding the herd and taking great care to keep the wind at my face, so that it doesn't carry my scent toward the animals. From my hiding place I cannot see the sciapod, but I know that he is there, at this moment dragging himself along the ground until he is close enough. The pegasuses stir nervously, they sense something, so when my friend gets up and bounds toward them, advancing five meters with every hop on his enormous leg, they all begin to fly. As we suspected, the male leader does not take off yet, but rather faces down the sciapod to guard the herd's departure and to try and knock him down with his powerful wings and hooves, but meanwhile I have run toward him as fast as my legs can carry me. When the winged horse discovers me, I am already very close. He extends his wings but, with a speed that would have been impossible for me before eating the manticore heart, I reach him before his hooves can leave the ground and latch onto his mane. With much difficulty and all of the strength of my arms, I boost myself and scale his back all while he struggles to take off. Then he tries to buck me off, doing pirouettes in flight that would have knocked me off a dozen times over if I did not have for today the strength of that archer-predator. Seeing that he cannot buck me, he heads toward the forest and flies through the thicket, whose branches rend deep furrows in my back. But I hold tight and, five minutes later, the winged horse surrenders and allows me to lead. I direct him toward the plateau, careful to keep enough distance between us and the crags where dwell the harpies who could shoot us down with their arrows.

The ascent takes half an hour, thirty minutes of absolute freedom during which the wind rushes over me and I can gaze out across the enormous plains, the herds of centaurs, the forests, and the fields of thinking flowers. Further off, the Sea of Sirens, with whom I lived in the city of Triton for a couple months in another stage of my long journey. The low-lying clouds grow closer and then engulf us. The chill makes me shiver; perhaps I should have covered myself in skins, but nudity is the custom of most peoples in the land, and I did not want to seem stranger than I already am. When the clouds retreat, I see that we have already reached the top. We are flying now through a region replete with fumaroles where the fire giants live, a species famous for their irascible nature and one that I count among those that I never want to meet, which is why I keep the pegasus aloft by tugging on his mane. What's more, the animal has already gotten used to me and he doesn't seem uncomfortable with my weight, so I decide to fly to the end of this leg instead of descending into such an inhospitable place.

The arid volcanic region gives way to cloudy forests woven with pines, willows, and oaks, among which are sure to be talking trees. Finally, I see fires that do not surge from the earth but rather rise from firewood: the settlement of cynocephali to which I am headed. Above it, on top of the mountain, I manage to make out a brilliant white light that tells me that there I will encounter the temple which motivated this entire journey. At last I contemplate the final destination of this voyage which began over a year ago. But it will not end today. Today I will simply present myself in the city.

I dismount from the pegasus in a clearing half a kilometer from the town. After I do so, I pet his muzzle. For a moment, I debate keeping him; once tamed the animal will not leave my side unless I free him. But it would be discourteous given how much I owe to him. Moreover, his herd needs a leader and a being as solitary as me could not be forgiven for hoarding him away from his own kind. Besides, I do not intend to return whence I came. So, instead of keeping him, I take one of his wings in my hand and extract a black feather. The pegasus whinnies, upset at the treatment, but he allows it. I stow the feather in a pocket of the leather bandolier made by the dwarves which constitutes the entirety of my raiment and where I keep other treasures from my journey, like the lock of hair from that siren who loved me for a week, the poem that the elves gave me, or what I have left of that cicatrizant bark which I should apply later to mend the gashes left by the branches. After this, I express my thanks to the pegasus for transporting me, whispering into his ear and then slapping him on the rump. Sensing that this is the ritual to free him, the winged horse takes off. He will return to his own kind, but he will remember my scent. The bond has been forged: if we meet again sometime, he will let me ride him.

Watching him go, already thinking of him as yet another friend that I have dismissed on this long journey, I ask myself how many beings I have come to know these past two years… and consider my essential solitude. During all this time I have seen many beings similar to me in some form or another, but always with some difference so great that I cannot be considered part of their people. Centaurs, satyrs, elves, dwarves, sirens. Always in communities, always more than one. I am the exception. Are they variations of me or I of them? Am I perhaps a mutant offspring of one of these races? And if this is not so, where are my own people? Have I been born simply to be always alone?… Through the trees, I contemplate the temple and wonder if I will find answers there.

I walk unhurriedly toward the town. The afternoon is well on its way, but nightfall will not reach me before I arrive and I will not ascend to the temple anytime before tomorrow. When I come upon the first houses, their solidity surprises me. I have not encountered many permanent settlements on my journey. Only among the elves, the most ancient of all beings, have I seen a city larger or better-constructed. The streets of the town are wide, paved with stone, and to one side the rumor of an aqueduct can be heard. The cynocephali are obviously industrious. Many of them are in the street and I observe how some keep their body nude and others cover it with fabric vestments.

There does not seem to be any more convention to it than the desire of each individual or the cold that they feel. In the doorway of one of the houses, a mother plays with a girl. The girl is lovely; she laughs with her little canine face and wags her tail happily. In every other aspect she is identical to me—that is, if I were female. It makes me think of some other beings, a little less peaceful; the minotaurs, with whom I enjoyed more than a couple drunken benders little over half a year ago. They also had a body similar to mine and a face that was completely alien, although now, in lieu of taurine features, they are canine.

Off to one side of the mother and daughter, a male cynocephalus observes the scene with satisfaction. The pair seem trustworthy, so I approach them and bring my hand to my mouth, indicating to them with this universal gesture that I'm hungry, because aside from the manticore's heart, I have not had a bite to eat all day. The male gazes at me for a moment, studying my face; he also fixates with curiosity on the iridescent colors of my member, courtesy of the wac-wac sapling. Obviously, as always, I am the first of my species that he has seen. He takes a deep whiff of me, discretely, from a distance, but I see how his nostrils flare. Finally, he seems to decide that the trust is mutual, and gets up to show me a mountain of firewood to one side of the house. I assent and get to work.

While I chop and pile the wood, I say to myself that they must already be used to strange visitors who come to the temple, although, certainly, many more come than return. Retrieving the wood that I have split, I can't help but look at the rainbow which adorns me. In spite of all of the sweat of the day, the colors remain intact, just as vibrant as they were immediately after my floral copulation. I wonder if the stains will ever go away.

When I finish it is already nighttime. The cynocephalus directs me to a hut and hands me clothes made of a material that I cannot identify, not leather but some sort of cloth. In the hut a bathtub filled with hot water awaits me… a luxury that I have only experienced among the elves. I wash myself carefully and stay in the water until it begins to get cold. After drying off, I take a piece of the sylvan bark that the nymphs gave to me after that unforgettable fête and rub my wounds from the day. By tomorrow they will have healed over.

I return to the house. The cynocephalus awaits me there with his family, among whom I now notice another pair of members. Seated on a great chair: a grandfather in whose face, salted with white hairs, are worn many decades of experience, and a puppy just learning to crawl. He has an adorable little face and the girl keeps leaning over to rub his head, to which he responds by wagging his tail happily. It is a lovely family, I say to myself, as I take my seat at the table with them; the refinement of this advanced society is such that they even have furniture. It gives me pleasure to spend the night in their company. In addition, the food is delicious: buffalo meat lightly grilled and seasoned in a manner I do not recognize. Taking a bite, I note that it is cooked perfectly: my teeth meet resistance at the seared flesh, but within I can taste the gush of blood and savor the tenderness.

They give me a blanket and indicate a place on the floor for me to sleep. I see that this is the custom, since they all take their places in different parts of the house. The two kids curl up side by side, their bodies all jumbled together, and their laughter resounding like stifled barks. As I try to fall asleep, I think about the journey and about the temple. I have no memories beyond the moment two years ago when I awoke in the rainforest where the wise monkeys found me and adopted me as one of their own, and I spent more than a year traveling before I found out about the existence of the temple. I know what tomorrow has in store for me, but today, when I have almost reached my goal, I doubt whether I should complete what little remains. What sparks this doubt is not the sphinx that awaits at the top of the long steps. Nor is it the fear of failing to provide the answer she will demand in order to let me pass, and the certainty of being devoured if I fail. No, it is not that; I have come through too much danger in my wanderings to be intimidated by that. And I know that once I pass that final test, I will be able to ask the Hermaphrodite Angel that lives in the temple about the mysteries which compelled me to travel. No, it is not any of that: it is just that as I watch this sleeping family, I question whether I should not find some way to remain here. Or at least to prolong my stay. After all, if there is one thing I can count on, it is that the temple isn't going anywhere. Yes, today I am not sure if it is worth it to ask the Angel where I come from or if there are others like me. Today I question if it is really so bad to be different.

Tomorrow I will see. Tomorrow I will ponder and decide. For now, I am too tired to do anything but sleep. So I wish for peaceful dreams and, without further hesitation, close my eyes.

ABOUT THE AUTHOR

Andrés García Londoño is a Colombian-Venezuelan writer. He was born in Caracas in 1973, grew up and lived most of his life in Colombia, and has lived for the last decade in the City of Brotherly Love, Philadelphia. *Hybrid Vigils* is his first book translated into English, but he has published three books in Spanish to date: *Los Exiliados de la Arena* (2001: short stories), *El Caballo de Ulises: una Reflexión sobre la Utilidad de la Literatura* (2006: essay), and *Relatos Híbridos* (2009: short stories). The last one, which was translated as *Hybrid Vigils*, was written after winning a scholarship contest for literary creation conducted by the Office of the Mayor of Medellín. He has also published over twenty long-form articles, and over a hundred short articles and book reviews in academic and literary journals in Latin America and the U.S. He has a degree in Communications from the University of Antioquia and a Master of Arts from the University of Pennsylvania, where he currently is finishing his Ph.D. in Hispanic Studies and teaches courses on Spanish language and Latin American history and literature.

ABOUT THE TRANSLATOR

Taylor Brady is a translator, structural engineer, and lyric poet from Tucson, Arizona. He has published co-translations of short stories and novellas in different journals and magazines, including *Metamorphoses* and *Modern Chinese Literature and Culture*. *Hybrid Vigils* is his first book-length solo translation. He holds a B.S. in Civil Engineering and an M.S. in Structural Engineering and Geomechanics from Stanford University, and is a licensed professional engineer in the State of California. He is broadly interested in literature written from the margins of hegemonic cultures, critiques of technocratic determinism, and literature of the American Southwest. At present, he is translating a trilogy of Colombian novels into English and studying for his structural engineering (S.E.) licensure exam, assisted by his all-black cat apprentice: Cat Lord Eboshi, E.I.T.